To Mike &

Nic Carey was born in Wokingham, Berkshire, in 1952 but spent his formative years in Paignton, Devon, before going to Manchester University and qualifying as an architect. Having spent 12 years in Canada, he is now retired and lives in Gozo with his wife, Dolores, and their three dogs. He is a member of the Rotary Club of Gozo and active in the community, particularly with the elderly and disabled. Nic has a daughter who is an interior designer and a nephew who is an author in Bogota, Colombia.

Best wishes

Nic

PS. Do not read Synopsis if you don't want to know the end!

Dedicated to my wife, Dolores, without whom this would never have been written; and to my daughter, with love.

Nic Carey

THE BOY WHO TALKS TO ANIMALS

AUSTIN MACAULEY PUBLISHERS™

LONDON • CAMBRIDGE • NEW YORK • SHARJAH

A CIP catalogue record for this title is available from the British Library.

ISBN 9781528981743 (Paperback)
ISBN 9781528981750 (ePub e-book)

www.austinmacauley.com

First Published (2019)
Austin Macauley Publishers Ltd
25 Canada Square
Canary Wharf
London
E14 5LQ

I would like to acknowledge the people at Paignton Zoo and all those who really care about the protection of our wildlife.

Table of Contents

Synopsis   **11**

Introduction   **15**

Chapter 1   **17**

Noise in the Night

Chapter 2   **25**

A Strange Occurrence

Chapter 3   **38**

Much Ado About a Lot

Chapter 4   **47**

Betrayal – A Fool's Game

Chapter 5   **68**

The Great Escape

Chapter 6   **80**

A Plan is Formed

Chapter 7   **93**

Swimming in Mud

Chapter 8   103

Life Changes

Chapter 9   120

Resolution and Weirdness

Chapter 10   130

The Legend of the Feyr

Chapter 11   143

Winds of Change

Chapter 12   160

Fame – A Two-Edged Sword

Chapter 13   175

Disaster Strikes

Chapter 14   186

The Awakening

Chapter 15   197

The House on the Moor

Chapter 16   208

A Child of God

Epilogue   214

Synopsis

Friends and family are why I wanted to write this book. My answers ranged from "I'm not sure" to "I just had to". The question was what genre is it? Answer – several. It has elements of humour, sadness, mystery and romance. Probably, the most interesting aspect is the way it was written – in my sleep. As a designer, I have often problem-solved while asleep and then woken up to put a workable solution down on paper. This was exactly that, except me having to use three out of my ten fingers instead on the keyboard!

Strangely, or not, this led to one of the main aspects of this book and that is the possible latent abilities we all have inside us, untapped, unsourced and for us all, maybe, lost in time. Those "Ancients" knew a thing or two!

The setting of this book is a provincial zoo in the south west of England where I grew up. The location is real; the characters are not. The book is both anecdotal and conversational. There are many passages dispersed throughout the book, detailing various experiences with individual animals; explanations on the workings of the zoo for context and some of my sillier jokes.

The main characters are one of the deputy head keepers and a young boy whom he finds is living in the zoo unknown to anyone. He finally traps the boy one night and finds that understands but that he will not or cannot speak. He is dressed in near rags and has no identification.

Alarmed by potential bad press but curious about the boy's empathy with the animals, the zoo agrees that he can stay there in their temporary accommodation until they can find out where he comes from.

Unfortunately, the other deputy head keeper informs the police and social services and the boy is taken off to a children's home where he causes mayhem. In desperation, social services decide agree to let him stay in the zoo while enquiries are made under a temporary protection order.

As the days pass, it becomes very apparent that there is a lot more to the boy's abilities than simple empathy and it is found that he can actually communicate with animals. He does this by sound but cannot speak.

The head keeper and his wife, Molly (who is head of the Catering Department), offer him a place in their home nearby to placate social services which is accepted. However, each night he leaves and goes to the main island in the middle of the lake to stay with the Lar Gibbons. He has repeatedly asked his name with no response so he is offered a list and chooses "Larry".

Molly is from a village on the nearby moor and professes to have some insight into the boy's abilities. She and her husband, Joe, take Ben to a lifelong friend who is a retired professor of social anthropology who explains about some of the legends on the moor and his theory of the origin of the "special people".

Time goes on and Larry becomes a very useful part of the education programme at the zoo. This includes demonstrating a variety of live animals to school parties and visitors under the guidance of the very lovely Cecilia who has joined the staff.

This attracts the attention of not only Ben, the deputy head keeper, but the press. Larry's fame is further enhanced when he rescues a young boy who has fallen into the leopard enclosure. The notoriety escalates from the local press to the national press to regional television.

Other people have been alerted and staff at the zoo, following a break-in, are aware of two men who are acting suspiciously. The Professor warns about the people and gives further explanations of whom they may be and what they are after. It is agreed that a tight watch should be put on Larry as a similar child many years previously had been spirited away never to be seen again.

Larry is innocent and naïve and is lured away by the strangers and a massive hunt ensues but he cannot be found. An idea is put forward as it transpires that the Professor, himself, was born on the moor and has a secret ability which he keeps hidden for fear of it getting into the wrong hands. He tells the story of the little girl he played with as a boy in that village. She had also attracted attention at the local fete, as she apparently had possessed the ability to make plants and crops flourish.

The Professor is able to find the boy and determine his condition and immediate environment but not the location.

A meeting is held at his cottage and a sort of séance is conducted designed to amplify his ability which is successful. Then the question of his location is answered through Molly and the spot where he is being held is dowsed on a map.

Molly and Cecilia are left at the cottage, and the three men travel to the area they have pinpointed. While parked there, the Professor sees an older woman whom he recognises from his youth. She is the girl that disappeared. Realising that they have found the house and that their privacy is prejudiced, she takes them to the remote house and they meet the "Watchers" who are father and son who have a sacred duty to source and protect the "special people". The son is childless and his wife barren so they wish to keep the boy and train him to succeed them to maintain the rite.

The boy is in a bad way and kept in a locked room. He will not eat and is ill. The three men tell the Watchers that if they do not give him up voluntarily, they will inform social services (under whom he is already protected) and the police with a charge of kidnapping.

The watchers under pressure, as well by their wives who are concerned about the child's well-being, reluctantly agree and Larry is returned to the zoo.

Sadly, incarceration and malnutrition have taken their toll and Larry develops a bad cough leading to pneumonia. Early one morning, unusual events are happening at the zoo. Police have been called about excess noise from all the animals and suddenly, they go quiet. Larry has passed away.

Paperwork is quickly sorted out and permission is given for Larry to be laid to rest on the island being the place he loved best.

The people close to him find they have special abilities which he has helped to awaken in them.

I hope you enjoy reading it as much as I have enjoyed writing it.

Best wishes,
Nic

Introduction

Ever since I was a young boy, I have always had a passion for animals and all I ever wanted was to work with them in some way. Luckily, I grew up in a small provincial town by the sea which had a zoo. Not only a zoo, but sea life aquaria, sanctuaries for otters and hedgehogs, a butterfly farm and of course the nature all around.

I joined the zoo club at an early age which heightened my interest even more. We were not only taught about different animals and their behaviour but were schooled in their care, diets and health.

My father asked me when I was eight years old, 'Ben, what do you want to be when you are older?'

'A keeper at the zoo, Dad,' I replied.

Apparently, at that age, all boys wanted to be train drivers, explorers or zookeepers, so my father ruefully shook his head and no doubt thought that I would grow out of it and choose a "proper" job.

I didn't.

The zoo was unusual. Built in a green valley heavy with trees, it was of abnormal size compared with other zoos. This afforded a great deal of space and privacy for animals but the downside was some discontent from visitors who would peer myopically into enclosures hoping for just a glimpse of its contents only to be disappointed.

The larger animals were more easily viewed while others were only known to be alive as their food disappeared or if one could sit very quietly and patiently to catch a glimpse.

As time passed by, the zoo grew in stature and became (and still is) best known for its preservation of endangered species and breeding programme. My involvement increase to a formal part-time basis; then a keeper and finally, now, to a deputy head keeper.

Little did I realise of the strange and unique events that would follow.

Chapter 1
Noise in the Night

Taking care of animals is a twenty-four hour job. Looking after animals with an active breeding programme is even more taxing so staff have to spend many a long night at the zoo. Some slept in the temporary bunks or played cards or watched TV but for me, night was a magical time. No hustle and bustle of visitors and a whole different range of noises from the nocturnal and semi nocturnal animals. I would wander around the zoo listening to the sleep sounds and every now and then, an inquisitive face would appear as a nice surprise.

That particular night, it was my turn to look after Blimp. Blimp was an elderly orangutan who had been saved from poachers in Sumatra at an early age and was a great favourite in the zoo. Sadly, being orphaned, part of his upbringing and training was lacking and he had never got full confidence in swinging through the trees. This had inevitably ended up with several injuries, the latest being a dislocated and twisted shoulder.

So, Blimp was happily in post-operative bliss and snoring as only orangutans can and believe me, they can!

It was during this balmy night in July when a bit tired of the sounds of Blimp and the accompanying body expulsions that I went out for a wander for a few minutes.

The centre of the zoo contained a restaurant overlooking a small lake and Gibbon Island. The smell of burgers, chips and fat fryers pervaded. An unwelcome change to the heady "farmyard" smells of the rest of the zoo. Then suddenly, noises.

A clatter of metal; a squeak like fingernails on glass and a moan that did not sound human.

Looking through the panoramic glass window, I could see a stainless steel trolley overturned but no sign of the cause. Certainly, it was not something that could fall over by itself or be toppled by any small creature. No sign of entry, back or front so a mystery.

The following day, I am on a late shift and decided to investigate further as it was bugging me. I went in to speak to Molly.

Molly is a sixty something-ish, largish, sweetheart who is in charge of all catering and has been at the zoo forever. There is a theory that she was in fact the first exhibit. We told her she was zaftig to soften her physical description and to appease her as she does feed us but she says she cannot spell it so just fat will do!

'Hello, my luvver,' she said. Now this needs a bit of explanation as anywhere else in the country, this would be taken for a "come-on" at best or invitation to pay for certain services at worse. Here, however, in Devon, it is a normal form of greeting from a lady to a man. Many are caught out by this and Molly herself says she has had many dinner invitations from visitors because of it. She adds that most are disappointed. Not quite sure what she means by this as it could be taken two ways so best left alone as, as I said, she feeds us. We all adore Molly.

'Molly, I heard a crash last night. Place was locked up but I could see the tray trolley had fallen over. Then there were some other noises.'

'Yes,' she said, 'I really don't know what happened. We had the kitchen company here yesterday doing their annual steam clean, so they may have left it a bit unbalanced. This is the only time I ever lock up as these guys use some funny chemicals and they always tell me to leave the place clear for twelve hours or so.'

'Funnily enough, though, I have noticed a few things lately that were not where I left them so I assumed it was you lot having your midnight nibbles and not clearing up after yourselves. As for last night, I have no idea. Anyway, as there were no food leftovers on account of the cleaning operation, I have made you a special supper.'

'OK, my luvver, see you later and I will leave your supper in the oven, as I am going home in an hour.'

With that, I left and went off to the penguin enclosure further up the main track passing the lake and Gibbon Island on the way.

Gibbons are strangely quiet this evening, I thought, usually there is some hooting going on and a bit of rough-housing in the trees at this time before they settle down for the night. Now, Gibbons, like most monkeys and apes, are not keen on water. With Gibbons, it is almost a paranoia, so this colony lives on a small island in the middle of a lake. We have a little rowboat to get to the island although most of the time, it is easier just to wade across the thirty feet of thigh-high water.

One of our "student" keeper had the bright idea to do away with the boat and spent many hours constructing a raft which you pulled on a rope suspended from two trees on either side of the water.

Estimates are never exact which is why they are called estimates, but we think the gibbons worked it out in less than two hours but we it took us a good eight hours to round them up from all around the zoo and beyond. They were having a great time except one who was being held at bay by an irate, black swan and a young gibbon who had found his way into a neighbour's greenhouse and was very content eating anything in there, particularly his prize tomatoes.

He came quietly. Bloated but quiet. I don't think he was feeling too well.

So, some restitution was paid to the neighbour who luckily was quite amused by the whole episode.

Gibbons were taken back in ones and twos to the island but in doing so, one more returnee was in the process of leaving the island. As we watched, we could see what was happening. The process was remarkably simple. They just hung on the rope and went hand over hand until they reached the other side. Once one had worked it out, there was no stopping them.

The following day, the little rowboat was pulled out of the bushes; the rope removed and the little raft moored on the lakeside. The status quo had been re-established, fun time was over and all was well again apart from a few days of gibbon sulking. Not sure what happened to the student, but he finished out the rest of his placement very quietly!

Animal escape was always an issue. Some local residents did not like the zoo because of the noise and smells. Some had an unrealistic phobia that they would be gored by an escaping camel in the middle of the night. One had actually got out and was caught some two miles away just off the main road to the neighbouring town.

As I told the reporter, camels do not gore, they would spit and bite or just trample you to death besides, they are too tall to get through a front door. I also told them in a flippant moment that camels have a very strong homing instinct and this one was trying to get back to Libya.

In true editorial fashion, the local paper printed the story and complete with the headline "LIBYAN CAMEL HEADS HOME". Needless to say, the zoo were not impressed and I was told that I had been banned from having any contact with the media in future and any announcements were to be handled by the press officer. *Interesting,* I thought, as I didn't know we even had a press officer but as things stood, it was best to keep that to myself.

Not all the escapees were unpopular. A large number of exotic birds had escaped over the years and some were now even breeding. It was not unusual to see a flock a brightly coloured birds of all species flying around the town. However, anything larger was definitely not acceptable.

The main perpetrators were the monkeys, apes, lemurs and worst of all, the raccoons. Some real escape artists among them but in general, they would not go far as many were kind of institutionalised, and they would panic if too far away from home ground.

The zoo was very much run on a tight budget and of course, animal welfare was the priority. Security was an expense which the zoo felt was an extravagance and besides, there were always staff on site day and night. Who would want to break into a zoo anyway? What was there to steal – a warthog, couple of parrots? However, there was always the risk of a bit of devilment fuelled by an excess of alcohol, so we were asked be aware.

After checking the penguins who were all happily huddled in penguin coma with not even a beak being raised to my presence, I toddled off to the restaurant for my promised supper. As usual, the restaurant door was open; the low oven light on and the oven door slightly ajar.

There was no food.

Now, this was a first, when Molly said she would do something, you could put your life on it so there must be another explanation. I was the only person on duty that night so there was no one else who could have eaten my supper. I had to investigate.

Now, as I said, the front door was left open and this led onto an outside picnic terrace looking over the main track and the lake beyond. This was probably the best-lit area in the whole zoo, as other areas were kept dark on purpose so as not to confuse the animals as to whether it was day or night. I decided to look around the back, as there were no windows or doors on the side of the building.

The rear area contained a large bin area where waste food was collected and recycled mostly for the omnivores. A rear door from this area gave access to the kitchen, but this was shut and locked. There were four small high-level windows; three which gave some natural light to the kitchen preparation area and a fourth to the dry storeroom.

All the windows were shut, but there was a slight opening in the fourth window and as I examined it further, I could see a small twig sticking out of the corner. A further search found a plate with the remains of some scraps of food on it.

So, it looks like the mystery had been solved and I wondered whether this had also been the source of the noises I had heard the night before.

Someone must have been pretty agile to be able to climb up on a wheelie bin and crawl through a pre-prepared window opening then presumably down the racking on the other side.

This person clearly did not want to be seen or they would have used the main door.

The end of my night shift coincided with the arrival of Molly who always came in early to start the preparations before the rest of her staff arrived. So, I told her what I had found.

'Well, my luvver, first thing is take that stick out of the window so this blighter can't get back in there,' she said.

'No, I replied, I think it is best to leave it so we may find out who it is.'

'Could it be one of your staff?'

'No, if it was one of them, they would be taking things from the store not helping themselves to cooked food. We had one of them once, and I got rid of her very fast I can tell you.'

She walked around apparently deep in thought. 'I've been thinking,' she said. 'We leave some unused food out in the bain-maries for the following days, the only exception being the day before yesterday when we cleared everything out for the cleaners. If this person had been breaking in regularly, we would not necessarily have noticed, as there was plenty of cooked food available. Mind you, I have cleared up some bowls and forks and spoons and suchlike which I thought were you lot.

'Now it could be that as there was no food available that night that this person got really hungry and the only thing to eat was the meal I left for you. So, if this had not happened, this could have gone on and on and we would have been none the wiser.'

'OK, Molly, I'm going to have to report this to my boss, Joe, and no doubt he will have to speak to the general manager too. Someone roaming around this place at night in the dark could get hurt and they will want to find out how they are getting into the zoo in the first place.'

Instead of going home, I waited half an hour for Joe to arrive. In the meantime, I walked around the perimeter of the zoo to see if there were any likely places for a person to get in. It was "take your pick". We had already got used to people arriving via the back farm gate to avoid paying or even coming through the woods. This had been the subject of many a discussion with the conclusion that it would cost far more to secure the perimeter than what we were losing from the non-payers. So, the end result was that priority be given to the animal compounds for theirs and public safety.

Joe was the head keeper and he had held that position since it was handed down to him by his father who was Jo without an "e".

Now Joe was a man of few words but a huge heart mostly for the animals I have to say, whom he much preferred to people. People were to be tolerated, as they brought vital revenue to keep the place going but given a choice, he would have well done without them. Woe betides anyone who was found to be cruel to "his" animals or lax in their work. He had a vicious temper though thankfully, I never saw it.

I had known Joe for the sixteen years I had worked in the zoo. *He liked and respected me,* I thought, *only because I loved the animals.* Joe was always resplendent in his uniform and cap. White shirt and zoo tie, clean-shaven, hair trimmed and highly polished working boots. This was probably because all the mucky jobs were left to us! Joe was a big man with huge hands and a ready smile. An outdoors complexion with some freckles and a mop of unruly brown hair with some premature greying at the temples. Joe gave the first impression of being an ex-military man but all that worked with him knew that his life had been, and always would be, the zoo.

Jo Senior had retired three times and finally dropped dead of a stroke aged eighty-six in the giraffe enclosure and found the following morning by the then assistant keeper apparently, so I was told, with a beatific smile on his face. Good job it wasn't the lion enclosure, there wouldn't have been anything to bury.

'Joe, can I have a word, please?'

'Shouldn't you have gone home, my lad?'

'Yes, but there is something strange happening,' I said, 'so I have been waiting to report it to you.'

I then related what I had found and my suspicions so he insisted that I accompany him to the restaurant.

'Morning, Joe, morning, my luvver,' said Molly. 'Aren't you meant to have gone home? You've been here all night.'

'Yes, but Joe wants me to show him the problem.'

'You know about this then, Molly?'

'Yes, Joe. Ben discussed it with me first as this is my domain.' I might add here that there was a territorial relationship between Ben and Molly and each jealously guarded their independence.

'Right lad, you go off home and get some sleep because you are on night shift again tonight and I want you to keep your ears and eyes open. In the meantime, I will go and talk to Mr Whitlam so he knows what is going on.'

Chapter 2
A Strange Occurrence

'Nice to meet you, finally,' I said, as I switched the light on in the restaurant.

Before me, crouched in the corner was what I can only describe as a ragamuffin. He was probably around 12 years old or in his early teens with a mop of unkempt hair. He gazed back at me not really in fear but more in wariness and just the sort of picture you could imagine as having a rabbit caught in your car headlights. He certainly wasn't surprise or anxious enough to stop eating and immediately crammed another mouthful in of what looked like leftover lasagne.

I could see he was eyeing the distance to his escape route through the dry store, but I had positioned myself between him and it on purpose and taken the precaution of locking the main door to the patio.

This meeting was the culmination of several weeks of planning. First, I had to make sure that there was indeed something going on and it was not just my over-active imagination. Then there was another episode with Blimp who had to be stitched up after having been bitten by one or his "family" who obviously did not take kindly to be ousted from his temporary top spot while Blimp was recovering before. Unfortunately, the bite became sceptic and Blimp had to undergo more minor surgery and a heavy course of antibiotics.

After all this during his re-repatriation, he had to be watched for almost twenty-four hours a day to stop the same thing happening again.

So, I had been busy during my night shifts and we had had some new arrivals and departures to and fro other zoos to contend with. I had been liaising privately with Molly just to check whether there were any further activities and she confirmed that she had gone to the trouble of placing items in certain places on purpose and this was certainly a nightly occurrence.

I decided to set the trap myself one night rather than involve anyone else as, frankly, I did not know what I could be facing. My first thought was that it might be one of the higher-developed apes who had found a way out of the enclosure. I quickly dispelled this idea as if it had been one of them there would be one hell of a mess. If you doubt this, you should see the videos of our weekend chimps' tea parties!

The night I chose was nothing out of the ordinary except that it suited my schedule; I was on duty and without too much to do. So I settled down to wait and promptly dozed off.

In a semi-conscious state, I am not sure what and from where the first sound came, but I can only describe it as a sucking hiss. It turned out afterwards that it was the sound of the store window being opened and the neoprene window gasket coming unstuck. Then, a few stealthy noises and a dark shadow moved across the white tiling behind the servery area. I waited it must be said, somewhat impatiently, then sprang the surprise.

'Would you like to tell me your name and what you are doing here?' I said. Not very original but all I could come up with at the time. 'I have known that someone was coming in here at night and here you are.'

His head moved from side to side and I could see he was continuing to judge whether to make a bolt for it so I crouched down so as to try not to intimidate him, a trick I learned from dealing with timid animals.

Now I could see him more clearly, he was definitely not malnourished which was hardly surprising, as he had had the run of the kitchen for goodness knows how many weeks. He was of average height, brown hair and very bright, blue eyes. His forehead was puckered up in a frown come scowl, but he did not seem at all frightened by the sudden confrontation.

'Are you going to speak to me?' I said gently. 'There is no need to be frightened, I am just very curious to know who you are and what you are doing here.'

No answer. He remained perfectly still.

'Have you run away from somewhere? Is there anybody who I should contact to let them know you are safe? Where is your home? Would you like something more to eat?'

Still no answer. Just a steady gaze but his eyes had lost their initial wildness. I thought I was getting through.

In a moment of stupidity, I got up and moved over to the bain-maries. My thought was to tempt him with food. Well, it usually works with the zoo animals.

Wrong!

All I had done was re-opened his escape route and he didn't think twice but bolted through the open, dry storeroom door. I actually got a hand on his ankle as he clambered up the shelving, but it slipped away and he was out through the window before I could catch him.

Next morning, I waited again for Molly to come on duty and related the night's events to her.

'Well, my luvver,' she said, 'that's one mystery solved, now you may never know who he is.'

'I suppose so, Molly, but there are some strange pieces to this that do not add up.

'First, why the zoo, of all places except of course he may have found quite by chance that we are not too security conscious and that the food for him is free, unprotected and in huge quantity. He hasn't needed to steal anything from the store and take it away, as he can just get in and eat his fill.

'Second, he looks dirty and dishevelled but he seems quite comfortable with the way he has been living although to be fair, neither of us knows how long this has been going on.

'Third, I have absolutely no idea where he came from or who he is. He will not answer any of the questions I put to him and I am pretty sure he was not really afraid of me.

'Fourth, he had no shoes or socks on. I wondered whether he had taken them off to make less sound but by the state of his feet, I am not sure he has any.

'Fifth, I have looked all around the zoo for places to get in or to hide once inside to no avail. You know and I know that there are plenty of ways to avoid the front gate. I have looked in some of the old buildings and can find absolutely no trace.

'I am at a loss but in any event, I am going to have to report back to Joe and see what he wants to do about it if anything. For now, I am off to bed. See you tomorrow.'

'Wait a moment,' Molly hesitated in thought. 'I told you I was keeping my eyes open well I have. I know exactly what he has been eating and drinking. The "wild boy" theory doesn't fit somehow, as he is very tidy and leaves no mess. In fact, if I had not left some pointers out, I would not know he had been here. Except for one thing, water on the floor. Most of it in the dry store and then getting less as you go towards the servery. If he was dripping something he was drinking, then it should be the other way around. More water in the servery and less in the store.

'Food for thought, excuse the pun. Nighty-night.'

Twenty-four hours after this, I was back on day shifts and summoned to Joe's office having previously had a brief telephone conversation to him with my findings.

Before this, however, let me give you some insight into the zoo and how it was organised.

The zoo is a trust and therefore has a board of trustees kept somewhat in control by the chairman. I say somewhat in control as from time to time, we find trustees "helping" aka getting in our way but generally in a very genial way and he has the thankless task of putting that to them diplomatically.

Under the board is the general manager, Mr Geoffrey Whitlam (known as Walt and if you don't get that, then I am not going to enlighten you). Walt is a very busy man but a great organiser who works on the principle that you are paid to take responsibility so unless WW3 has broken out or a visitor has been seriously maimed by one of our animals, then we should deal with it. I think I am actually wrong there – scratch the animal bit, that would be our fault, just WW3.

The, there are several departments, each of which has a manager:

Molly, the catering manager, whom you have already sort of met.

The Administration Department who deal with reception services, shop staff and sales, franchising and very mundane stuff like accounts.

The Cleaning and Maintenance Department. They build things, repair things and clean public areas but are specifically excluded from inside the animal enclosures.

The Education and Marketing Department. They deal with school visits, adult lectures, the zoo club and zoo guiding: advertising events and visitor spectaculars.

Many of the staff in this department are unpaid helpers and many of them are very willing but not very able. Most of the zoo disasters are down to this department, take for example the Chimps Tea Party. This is a great favourite among the visitors but can get easily out of hand. Correction – will get out of hand. We get fed up with trying to coax over-excited chimps down from trees or trying to placate some three-year-old (and worse her mother) who has just been pelted with some sloppy food mess and is threatening to sue. Other instances are the snake handling display where one escaped and it happened to be a hooded cobra. The presenter had just told the crowd how dangerous they were while taking her eye off it and it happened to wander (I mean slither) into the throng. If the presenter had a bit more wit about her, she would have first explained that it had been de-fanged. That would have reduced the hysteria somewhat. As it was, the stampede was a sight to behold.

I follow this with an even more foolhardy venture – the camel ride. Camels are not known for the amenable nature and this one of ours was one of the worst I have ever had the misfortune to deal with. Faced with two very annoying eight-year-olds on its back, one of whom was trying to fill its right ear with candyfloss, it decided to spit at the father who was not privy to the ways of this particular creature. It starts with a low gurgling noise where the camel starts to regurgitate a sticky, yellowish-green mass from deep inside itself. Then after masticating this for a bit (that's when the ears go back) and presumably picking its target, this glob is launched with surprising accuracy up to a dozen feet away. Did I mention it smells horrible as well?

Sorry, I got a bit carried away there.

Then of course the most important department of them all – The Keepers.

Joe is the head keeper with a nice hat with his title on it. We, the full-time keepers, have nice hats too but they are frankly a bloody nuisance and get sat on, crapped on, stolen by the monkeys or simply mislaid. We wear them for ceremonial occasions! Joe and I are very much alike so we get on very well and we share very similar opinions on a wide range of subjects.

Under Joe, there are two assistant or deputy keepers. One is me and the other is Spencer Wilks. Spencer will come into this story in due course but to put it politely, he is a "one-off". Spencer is tall and lanky with a long pinched nose and thin lips. He will never look you directly in the face and has what I call a shifty demeanour.

I forgot to mention. Bad memory! Spencer is Walt's nephew. Worse – Walt thinks that Spencer is brilliant and has a prodigious memory. Reluctantly, I have to admit that last bit is true but like a lot of automatons he does not seem to have the power of reasoning to go with it.

Now, when charisma or charm was given out, Spencer was absent and when the humour button was installed, Spencer was not even in the queue. With Spencer, everything had to be "by the book". Funnily enough, we did have a manual, I lost mine somewhere. Spencer not only has his it is memorised and he takes great delight in quoting from it from memory.

Saying all this and apart from his apparent lack of empathy with animals, or humans for that matter, if you ask Spencer to help, he is there and he has a prodigious knowledge about all creatures. Sometimes we see Spencer walking around looking depressed so we have a trick to buck him up.

'Mr Wilks, we have a lady here who is asking about the Galapagos Tortoise. Would you kindly enlighten her please because you know all there is to know about them.' Spencer would stick out his chest and strut, yes actually strut like a male peacock and proceed to bore the hell out of her for fifteen minutes. This would then keep him in good spirits until the depression took hold again and we would then find him another victim.

Privately, Joe and I have a nickname for Spencer. It's a kind of personal joke between us that I was responsible for. Joe heard me muttering under my breath something about Moby and enquired what I meant.

'It's my pet name for Spencer which I use when I am mad at him,' I said.

'Why Moby?' he asked.

'Have you read Herman Melville?'

'Who's he?'

'A writer.'

'What did he write?'

'A book.'

'Very funny, what's it called?'

'Moby Dick.'

A small rumbling sound started from somewhere deep down Joe's throat, accompanied by a sort of vertical shaking of the shoulders. I realised Joe had got it and there was a pent up eruption about to take place. And it did amid a sort of roaring-guffaw. Hard to describe.

'Moby Dick,' he spluttered. 'You got that right.'

'How is it you don't have a nickname, Joe? I said.

'I do,' he answered.

'What is it?'

'Joe,' he said smiling.

'So that's not your real name?'

'You're brighter than you look.'

'OK, what is it?' I asked.

'You had better not tell anyone.'

He stared at me for a few seconds.

'You promise? Aloysius,' he said quietly.

'Some parents are very mean, Joe.'

'Tell me about it, remember you promised.'

'I had my fingers crossed!'

Under us, the deputy head keepers, there are eight full-time keepers. They have nice hats as well. They each have their own particular duties which are mostly directly related to the animals they look after.

Next are the assistant keepers. These are a gaggle of low or unpaid students and learner keepers. Down from this are the volunteers who are generally more trouble than they are worth and often extricated from tricky situations by their peers.

To supplement this, there is a veterinary assistant, Freddy. His job is a sort of animal triage. If he can't handle the problem himself, he calls in the outside vet. The outside vet is here a lot!

Finally, there is Emily, the dietician. She is in charge of making sure animal food is purchased in the right quantity and quality and then prepares huge charts to tell the keepers what to feed to whom and when and how.

Emily has a close affiliation with the assistant vet, Freddy. In fact, a very close affiliation which they try to hide (for professional reasons). None of us is meant to know and of course, everyone does. I think it's her blushes that give it away any time she sees him or someone mentions his name or it could be the fact that when he has night duty, she then volunteers and can be found shredding vegetables to molecular proportion while she waits for the rest of us to vanish and presumably get to grips with Freddy.

I did ask her one day whether she was intending to feed the elephant with cabbage from a hypodermic but either she did not get it or more likely did not want it.

There, you now know the full contingent that make up the zoo personnel and there are a lot of them. Never counted them, but Accounts will tell you if you want, but I suspect it is in the region of fortyish full time employees; another forty part-time and seasonal staff and then a countless volunteers who come and go. As they are not given any form of uniform, they can be recognised by a yellow scarf worn like a boy scouts with a woggle.

They then are known as the Rabble. The yellow scarves are actually a warning sign for us and even some of the animals show signs of apprehension when they approach. I remember one zebra who would start braying and bucking around the paddock any time one of the Rabble came near.

Enough digression, but at least it has given you some insight into our little community. Best of all, every day is different and there is never a dull moment. The pay is awful but I would not be anywhere else.

It has been about four or five days since the "encounter" and according to Molly, the nighttime invasions have continued unabated. So, my conclusion is that I did not frighten the bejabers out of him and that he has found a comfy and safe haven where he is unlikely to be caught or rescued or whatever.

There was one point that Molly raised that has been nagging at me though about the water on the kitchen floor and also the fact that we had never determined where he was living. I am no Sherlock Holmes so the possible options had taken a lot of brainpower without any real workable theories.

I had established that he either had no footwear or he took them off to reduce any noise. Then the water on the floor. Then I remembered grabbing his ankle as he tried to get through the window and yes, his trouser leg was wet. As there was no rain that night, then he must have crossed water somehow.

I think I mentioned that the zoo had been built in a valley and from the top of the hill, a stream ran down into the main lake on which Gibbon Island stands. From there, a wider stream runs out into another lake which has a visitor feature in its centre and accessed by two rope bridges. This is where the lemurs live and they roam around freely much to the pleasure of the tourists until some fool tries to pick one up.

Two more streams join near the lake outlet and supplement an increasing volume of water which in turn feeds the flamingo pond next to the main entrance gate. The excess disappears via a mesh outlet into a large storm culvert which discharges across the main road somewhere.

I started tracing these waterways back to source and doing a quasi-Indian tracking thing looking for footprints. I have seen this several times in the TV and it is remarkably simple. You stare at a lump of mud, lightly massage some faecal droppings in your hand, put your ear to the ground and you are meant to be able to tell when and how many people went past even what they were wearing.

And, I believed it!

Complete waste of time but interesting how many non-zoo animals used the woods but as for our young intruder, I was none the wiser.

There was an interesting pile of cloths and sacking under the lemur house but they had been there for some time and I think this may have more to do with our own lovers' trysts than what I was looking for. I started again at the top of the hill even invaded some local residents' sheds and outbuildings and then back down the hill to the main lake and sat down.

The sides of the lake are grassed but there is one area where the boat is moored that has solid edge made from an old wooden telegraph pole. The boat is tied to a metal ring screwed into the pole. The pole itself is designed to help you get into the boat without sliding down or creating a muddy bank.

The edge of the lake is all grassed and a downstream weir guarantees a constant level of water even during or after a downpour. The many ducks and geese that live on the waterways within the zoo happily paddle around and hop in and out much to the amusement of the sometimes-bored gibbons who try to grab a passing fowl. They do not hurt them and it is done out of sheer devilment. One of them over-reached one day and actually fell into the water. I know, as I was the one that had to fish her out. Totally hysterical, she spent a long time in gibbon therapy and would not go within six feet of the water thereafter. She would even look at the water trough with deep suspicion.

I remember that at the time, thinking the silly creature was actually drowning, I launched into a dive fully clothed and promptly hit the bottom. It was only about eighteen inches deep (forty-five centimetres to you metric souls).

Could it be that the water came from the lake and this kid had been actually hiding on the island until he felt the coast was clear? It was certainly the best I had come up with and explained the lack of shoes, wet clothing, water trail on the floor and the fact I could not find him anywhere else. So, my theory was that he would get on to the island somehow and wait until dark then wade across and enter by his pre-prepared entry through the dry store window. As he got further into the building, he would drip less and less thereby leaving a confusing trail.

This all fitted so how then did he get on to the island in broad daylight or at least at dusk to await the full darkness. Maybe the island has some answers, so I decided to take the little boat over to the gibbon sanctuary. Two or three swift strokes were all it took to a similar mooring position on the island bank.

The island is about fifty metres in length and thirty wide with an assortment of tall deciduous and not so tall, evergreen trees and shrubs. Just off centre is the colony HQ which consists of a large semi-enclosed hut on stilts with a smaller "tree house" above it. There are two other small tree houses at either end of the island for those inmates who may not be feeling very sociable or have been ostracised (usually temporarily) for gibbon-misdemeanours by the others. Water was fed by a hose to a trough in front of the main hut which was a feature implemented after the semi-drowning gibbon episode.

Now gibbons are generally shy creatures and it is the zoo's policy not to treat animals as pets wherever possible so access onto the island would inevitably result in one thing. The gibbons would head for the safety of the tallest trees on the island then keep absolutely still and try to be invisible until the "danger" had gone.

This time, though, a strange thing happened. The younger ones took to the trees immediately and sat there not in silence as usual but making their gentle hooting sounds. I don't speak gibbon, but it was not sounds they make when they are being aggressive or frightened so it was very much out of character. What was even more surprising was that many of the adults had not taken to the trees at all but were sitting on the roof of the main hut and also making strange quiet noises.

I peered around the hut entrance and almost recoiled in amazement as just inside I could see a pair of bare feet. Here was the boy. He must have waded across the lake when no one was looking, crawled into the hut and fallen asleep waiting for his nightly sojourn.

Even more amazing, suddenly two cream and black faces appeared around the doorway so there were actually two adult gibbons in there with him.

Now gibbons are not aggressive creatures unless cornered or fearful but I did not think they would take too kindly to an intruder. Saying that, I used to walk around the zoo sometimes with a baby gibbon hanging around my neck completely nonplussed by visitors as long as he or she was in contact with the person they trust. Try to prise them off in an unfamiliar environment or by some stranger and all bets were off. Surprisingly strong and vocal, they kind of adhere to you and you would think you were struggling with an octopus and they can bite.

At this point, I did not know what to do. Should I wake him up? Would he be aggressive? How would the gibbons react? I decided to go for it and gently touched his leg. One of the gibbons then did a strange thing and mirrored my action by touching his other leg in almost a tender fashion. The boy started to wake up and the gibbon immediately put his arms around him in a way that reminded me of a mother protecting a child.

I asked him again what he was doing there and for his name and a string or useless questions to no avail. He just stared back at me with his arms around the gibbon.

Never seen anything like this before, I thought. The gibbons actually like him here and this must have been going on for some time, as there was a familiarity about the whole scene that was quite extraordinary. It was almost like they were protecting him in some way. That was why they had not reacted or behaved in their usual way. I must have sat there for several minutes, as I just did not know what to make of it when the silence was broken by a voice calling my name.

'Ben, what are you doing over there all this time, Joe wants to see you.'

'I won't be long,' I answered, 'tell him I'll be there in a few minutes.' Now, a normal reaction would be for the boy to run for the hills as quickly as he could once found out but none of it. As I got up from the hut threshold, he calmly lay back down presumably to go back to sleep.

So, I simply left him there.

Chapter 3
Much Ado About a Lot

'I think we have had to deal with some very unusual things here in my time, but this beats the lot,' so spoke Walt, the General Manager.

Joe and I had spent a considerable amount of time in his office the following morning filling Walt in with what had been going on. Joe had about the same level of curiosity as me and neither of us had any conclusions to give to Walt about what to do about it.

'Either of you got anything to suggest, because we can't just leave him there.'

'Sorry, Mr Whitlam, I don't.'

'How about you, Joe?'

'Geoffrey, I am still trying to get my head around this.'

Walt sat there for a few minutes and then, true to form, came out with his usual management strategy. If the first stage doesn't work (in this case, that is Joe and me), widen the area of responsibility to "dilute" the problem and share the load. Might have guessed.

'I presume you have not let Spencer in on this,' said Walt. 'Who else knows?'

'Well, I had to involve Molly because the evidence really came to light in her department,' I said.

'Quite right,' said Walt. 'Shouldn't upset Molly, key person, not a person to upset, did the right thing.'

Strange response, but I assumed there was some "history" between Walt and Molly. I will have to ask her about it sometime. Now is not the time.

The look between Joe and I answered Walt's question. 'Listen, you two. I know Spencer can be a bit awkward to deal with sometimes, but he is deputy head keeper and should be in on this. Besides, he might have some good ideas about a solution.'

There were three points I could have made about that sentence:

Spencer is indeed awkward – true.

Spencer is indeed deputy head keeper – also true.

Spencer might have some good ideas – extremely unlikely.

Walt pressed the button on his intercom to his secretary. 'Mabel, could you call Spencer on his walky-talky thingy and ask him to come here right away?'

Ten minutes elapsed while we all sat busily staring into space to await the arrival of Spencer.

A timid knock, then a furtive face appeared around the door.

'Yes, come in Spencer, we have a very strange situation to discuss and you need to be in on it.'

Over the next 10 minutes, Joe and I both briefed Spencer on the preceding events and as we did so, the furrows on his brow got deeper and deeper with disbelief. It just goes to show the state of my mind that while Joe was concluding the story, I was even imagining planting seed potatoes on his forehead. Surreal or what!

What came next was sadly predictable and I had real trouble trying to stifle a groan. Out came the rulebook. Moby true to form!

'This is disgraceful on several levels,' spat Spencer, luckily that with my experience with the camels, I had shifted position to make sure I was out of range. 'The boy should be arrested; he has broken into this zoo, stolen food and goodness knows what harm he has done to the gibbons.

'Then there is the liability. He might be mad; he might get ill and die. The rule book says…blah, blah…'

There is one thing you can say about Spencer, he definitely doesn't disappoint.

Walt interrupts the tirade which was building towards a crescendo, 'OK Spencer, we get your drift and you make some good points but let's keep clear heads about this. From what these two tell me, he is only a kid and far from harming the animals, the strange thing is that they seem to have taken to him.'

'No one thought to tell me what was going on,' said Spencer, trying to raise to his full height while seated and looking pretty ridiculous and obviously feeling hurt by being left out. With good reason.

By now, Spencer is fidgeting like he has some rodent down his trousers and his face has gone a rather strange colour between red and mauve. Looks like Spencer has more chance of pegging out than the boy at this rate!

But Spencer was not finished. 'And, what about our reputation,' he burbled, 'what is it going to look like if we let any Tom, Dick or Harry free access to the place. What if the press gets hold of this? I can see the headlines now.' Spencer got up and stared waving his arms around in a fervour.

'Zoo advertises sleepovers with the animals. Apply Now.
OR
Unsupervised child gets eaten by the lions
OR
Little girl gets torn apart by the baboons
OR...'

'Thank you, Spencer, we get your drift,' said Walt.

More like a bloody tsunami. Strewth. At this point, watching Spencer in full flow, whether he was actually a keeper or an inmate because his presence in the zoo must have saved the bulk of humanity from him for at least eight to ten hours a day.

The voice of reason broke in, 'Why don't we get the lad in without frightening him; clean him down as Ben says he smells a lot; treat him with some kindness and see what he has to say for himself,' said Joe.

Well said, Joe, I thought, *you have gone even higher in my estimation than before.*

'Look,' said Walt in characteristic fashion, 'you three go and see if you can find him. Take Molly with you as she is good with kids; the woman's touch, hey? Too many bodies with me there as well.'

As we walked out into the office yard, I got a particularly nasty look from Spencer. 'Not happy,' he said.

'You never are, Spencer, don't take this the wrong way. I didn't tell you (I lied), as I had to be sure I was not imagining things and didn't want to look stupid in front of you especially with your profound knowledge and experience.'

What a crawler, I thought, I nearly made myself sick with that one but it seemed to do the trick. Leave it to me. I know how to deal with Spence. Sadly, later events would prove me wrong on that one.

The colour had started to a rather more normal colour on Spencer's face and Joe had stuffed a rather unpleasant looking cloth in his mouth to stifle his reaction.

'Well,' he said, 'I'm glad you are making up. You were starting to behave like a pair of adolescent girls. How are we going to go about this? Do we converge on the island hoping he is still there and drag him off, or do we coax him from the shoreline with some "goodies"?'

'As he has not shown any alarm up to now, I think it safe to assume he will be still tucked up in the main hut on the island,' I said, 'so I think I should go across and waken him up gently then you two come across in the boat. What do you think?'

'Sounds like a plan,' said Joe.

'Don't agree,' said Spencer.

'What's your idea then?'

'We go the store and get the tranquilliser gun and a net. You coax him out and I will shoot him. Then we put him in the net and carry him to a spare cage. Be safer all around because you don't know how he is going to react.'

'For goodness sake, Spencer, he's just a kid, you can't go around shooting darts into people like that then locking them in cages. You were only talking about newspaper headlines a few minutes ago and now you seem intent on creating some more yourself. I can see it now:

'ZOO DRUGS AND KIDNAPS INNOCENT CHILD FOR THE WHITE SLAVE TRADE. IS THE ZOO THAT HARD UP?'

'All right, have it your own way, but I am not taking any responsibility for this.'

'You don't have to come with us if you don't want to, Spencer, I think we can manage one small human by ourselves,' said Joe.

'You are not going to get rid of me like that,' he said. 'I've got to see this. By the way, are we going to fetch Molly?'

'No, the boat is too small for the four of us anyway so let's see how we go on. If he decides to make a run for it, none of us are going to be able to catch him anyway.'

We were walking towards the lake when Spencer decided that he wanted to fetch something. 'I'll catch you up,' he said.

'He's up to something, Joe, I really worry about him sometime.'

A few moments later, we heard Spencer approaching us as a steady trot.

Spencer had his best jacket on; his hat and was carrying what looked like a cross between a walking stick and a cudgel.

'Spencer, I don't think that he is going to be very impressed with you in full uniform and what is the stick for?'

'He might get violent, it's for our protection.'

'For Christ's sake Spencer, are you nuts? Well, I suppose it's a step down from the tranquilliser gun.'

'Can't be too careful,' muttered Spencer.

'Here we are, I am going to take my boots and socks off, roll my trousers up and wade across. You wait here and come across when I signal. No shouting or doing anything to scare him. Spencer, are you listening?'

'Who put you in charge, Ben, let me remind you that I have been here longer and therefore your senior, so don't go giving me orders.'

'Calm down, Spencer,' said Joe. 'Ben's right, as he is the only person who has had contact with the boy.'

'It's just not right,' replied Spencer, sliding into a kind of grunge.

'Sorry you feel like that, Spencer, I'm not trying to upset you (I lied again) but there is no manual on this one. Now, can you see any activity on the island? I can see the main hut but not the other three smaller ones through the foliage. I can see part of the hut roof but no sign of any of the gibbons sitting on it as before. To tell the truth, I can't see any movement at all. So, here goes.'

Good job it is July as then water was quite warm and the bottom of the lake a sort of muddy slime without too many sharp or pointy pieces so the short journey across to the island was not unpleasant and without incident apart from a couple of Muscovy ducks who were rather over-interested but probably had some young around hiding in the bulrushes.

I was actually right in my first observation. There were no gibbons on the roof and the main hut was completely empty. I made a sort of helpless gesture to the other two waiting on the opposite bank and then a hand "stop" sign just in case they did not understand the first signal and decided to charge across.

Where is everyone and I made a long-practised soft hoot which normally produced a similar response from the gibbons. *Well,* I thought, *that's a relief, I can hear three replies so at least Spencer won't be able to think that the boy has run off with them.*

There were rustic ladders giving access to reach of the three upper tree houses. Not for the gibbons you understand, they do not need them. They were for the odd occasion that we needed to gain access to change bedding or check on the general well-being.

I climbed up the ladder very gingerly as they were not particularly robust to be met with a very unusual sight. Without counting them, I could tell that there were all the gibbons sitting in the branches quietly and in the middle of them – the boy.

Once again, he stared at me without fear or rancour so I gestured to him to climb down. He followed me down and sat on the threshold to the main hut.

'Will you talk to me?' I said very gently. He just looked at me. 'I have two friends over there who would like to meet you. Will you come across as I think it would be better than them coming over here and possibly scaring the gibbons? They are used to me but not so much to them.'

He considered this for a few seconds then gave a small nod. I shouted to Joe to bring the boat over to saver us wading back and he immediately started toward the island to pick us up. I could see Spencer standing on the bank, stick in hand.

'This is Joe,' I said, introducing the boy to him, 'he is in charge of all the animals here and he is a very kind man. You have nothing to fear from him.' *Wonderful speech,* I thought, *sounds a bit like "I come in peace" and about as useless.* However, there was just a glimmer of expression when I mentioned the animals so maybe he understands but either cannot or will not speak. One thing is for sure. He is an enigma.

'Let's the four of us go to the restaurant,' said Joe, 'The visitors have now gone and the zoo is closed so we will not be disturbed. Hopefully, Molly will still be there as she is usually first in and last out. The lad looks like he could eat something.'

'Hello, my luvvers,' the usual greeting, 'I see you have found our visitor. Hello, young man, what is your name?' No answer, so Molly put her arm around him to steer him towards one of the tables. Spencer scowled in the background but thankfully said nothing. I wished he would put the stick down.

Interesting reaction from the boy as he did not seem to mind our proximity and showed absolutely no signs of fear or discomfort.

'I will. Go and get him some food,' said Molly. 'Nothing like some good wholesome food to break down some barriers.'

Now to be inhospitable, I could take some issue with that statement as some of the food dished up here particularly the burgers could certainly break down barriers, walls, teeth and anything else. There was a joke that I dare not repeat, especially in front of Molly, that the new rhino enclosures were built out of ferrous concrete reinforced with two-day old burgers. Saying all that, it is a long time since I last tried one and it will be a long time before I am hungry or brave enough to try another.

The boy ate everything in front of him in a complete silence only broken by our futile attempts to engage him in some sort of conversation.

'Tell you what,' said Molly, 'we have a staff shower at the back here and there are some spare overalls he can have. I will give his clothes to the laundry girls. Not sure they are worth keeping but they may mean something to the lad. Can't do anything about shoes and socks though, but I will look in some of the empty lockers as sometimes they leave stuff behind. He can have a shower and you go and look for me. If the locker does not have a name on it, then it's fair game and you grab anything that looks useful. I will look after him and maybe give his hair a trim. Looks like he's got half a tree in there.'

'You give me and him an hour or so to clean up, I'll bleep you when we're ready.'

I had some tasks to carry out and it was getting dark so I left the restaurant on route to my next assignment and stopped to look at Gibbon Island and to muse on the events that day.

I am glad I did because I was met with another strange sight. I think mentioned the episode when I had to rescue one of the gibbons from drowning in the lake. Beth is her name and she is about thirty years old.

There she was sitting on the island by the lakeside and when I say sitting next to the lakeside, I mean with her feet practically in the water. The unusual thing about this was that due to her dunking her fear of water prevented her from coming within even six feet of the bank but there she was.

Even more peculiar, sitting alongside her, crouched in their normal gibbon fashion, were the rest of the gibbon colony all lined up on the bank and all staring toward the restaurant expectantly. Not a sound or movement among them.

Looks like they are waiting for something, I thought. *Very odd.*

It was over an hour and a half when my bleeper went off so I strolled back to the restaurant to be met at the door by Joe.

'You got the call then as well,' he said.

We went inside to be met by Molly and a smallish creature who I thought at first was a different person. He was certainly hard to recognise as the dirty little urchin we had left in her care.

He was washed and Molly had even cut his hair though not expertly, it was a definite improvement. She had produced the promised overalls, presumably a woman's judging by the fit and had even found a pair of old track shoes albeit several sizes too big.

'Say hello to the new man in my life, my luvvers, isn't he handsome? Trouble is, he won't tell me his name or where he comes from. I heard him making some noises in the shower but no words so I am none the wiser.'

The boy seemed quite comfortable with us and completely nonplussed by everything, so Molly said as it was late, he must be tired and we should look after him for a bit while she made him up a kind of cot in the staff locker room. It looked like the boy had brought out all of Molly's maternal genes so she was enjoying herself.

While we sat with him, he just stared out the window at the gibbons sitting in a line on the island and they stared straight back at him.

'You like the gibbons, don't you?' I said gently. 'They are my favourites.'

I may be imagining it but a different expression flashed across his face. He said nothing but the look said everything. There was an empathy here. It wasn't Tarzan and the jungle, it was something unreal.

Joe interrupted the moment, 'Time we left the lad alone for the night, we will have to take him to see Walt first thing in the morning. There are some decisions to make.'

Molly put her arm around the boy and led him away still looking over his shoulder for a last glimpse of the gibbons.

'You should say goodnight to the nice men,' she said. The boy said nothing.

God, I hope Moby is not here tomorrow, I prayed.

Chapter 4
Betrayal – A Fool's Game

I got to the zoo early the following morning, anxious and curious to see how the boy was getting on. Molly had the same idea. We went into his new "bedchamber".

'He's gone,' she cried, 'I tucked him in all nice and comfy.'

The track shoes were next to the cot, the blankets were rumpled, but apart from that, there no sign that he had even been there.

'Surely, he can't have just run off,' said Molly, obviously distressed.

'I will give you two guesses where he is, the shoes are the clue. Bet you he's back on the island. Let's go and see.'

We looked across at the island. I could count nine gibbons in the trees, some sitting quietly and some swinging around on the branches, but no sign of the other three. They could have been somewhere in the foliage so not a great concern. If you have ever been to a zoo, you will almost certainly see Lar Gibbons. They are a great favourite and one of several species. These come in different colours ranging from cream to beige to brown to black. They have abnormally long arms (well, not abnormal for them) and fairly short legs. Ungainly, when they are walking, they tend to hold their arms up in the air over their heads. In the trees, it is a different matter. Agile and graceful, they can move very from tree to tree faster than a man can walk.

Did I tell you they are my favourites, probably did. It is a great joy to go on their island with them as once they trust and get used to you they are surprisingly docile and affectionate. I have spent many an hour when I should have been better-occupied sitting on the island or watching them from the opposite bank under the pretext of studying their behaviour.

A shout to the island produced no reaction except for a small burst of hooting from the occupants in reply. So, I shouted again. This time a newly shaven head appeared around the door to the main hut. I was right.

Still no verbal reply from the boy, but at least a got a small wave. Two more heads appeared around the door and I could see these belonged to two of the lighter-coloured adult females.

'Are you coming here or do I have to come over there?' I shouted. *Silly question,* I thought. 'Hang on, I'm coming over.'

'Can I come too?' I had forgotten Molly was standing next to me.

'Probably not a good idea, Molly, the gibbons are quite shy and they scare easily. They are used to me but to them you are a stranger.'

'How is it then, that they can accept the lad but not me?' she said.

'That is what I want to find out.' Normally, if anything goes on to the island, it produces a cacophony of hoots and shrieks yet there he is not only on their island but seems to be completely accepted as one of them.

'Morning, Ben, morning, Molly.' Joe had arrived. 'What are you two up to?'

'Good morning, Joe.' If you look across there on the island, you may be able to spot a human hand hanging out of the main hut. On the end of that is our new addition. He seems to prefer sleeping with the gibbons than the very comfortable bed that Molly made up for him. We are just trying to work out why they seem to accept him without a murmur whereas anyone else they would be screaming the place down.

'Has he said anything?' said Joe.

'No, but I did get a sort of friendly wave off him but he seems to have gone back to sleep. There are at least two females in there with him that I have seen. The rest are all doing their usual gibbon stuff without an apparent care.'

48

'I came down here because we have been summoned,' said Joe, 'and we have to bring the lad with us so you had better go over and fetch him.'

'I was just about to do that. Hold the boat, will you, while I get in.'

'Oh! Molly, he wants to see you as well,' said Joe, 'as usual, the more the merrier.'

'Does that mean that Moby is invited as well?'

'Who's Moby?' asked Molly.

We enlightened her which set off a spasm of giggles and snorts. 'You got that right,' she added. Had I heard that phrase before?

I reached the opposite bank which is only separated by about forty feet of water within a few seconds, tied up the boat and went up to the main hut. The arm was in the same position so I assumed, correctly as it turned out, that he had fallen back asleep. I touched his arm and was immediately confronted by a pair of hostile eyes. Not his, but one of the adult females, who rushed across the hut, grabbed his other arm and started to pull him back into the hut.

I started talking quietly to the female and then another one appeared from somewhere deeper inside the hut and to my amazement, began to help to pull him inside.

'It's OK,' I said softly, 'I am not going to hurt him. You can let go.' I started to gently rub his arm as this is usually a placatory sign to gibbons, but the boy had woken up and started stroking the face of the first one which seemed to calm her down.

I have already told you that gibbons are not really aggressive creatures unless roused or frightened but to see a stranger doing this would usually be asking for a good bite.

Both females were now calm and I gestured to the boy to get up and follow me. The gibbons stayed in the hut door, watching us leave, joined now by the rest of the colony who were either uncharacteristically on the ground or sitting on the lowest branches.

As I held the boat and he got in, he turned and waved to them and they sat and stared without a sound as we departed.

'Hello, my luvver,' said Molly, as we landed, 'you didn't think much of the bed I made up for you.'

While I had been on the island, Molly had fetched his track shoes and made him a sandwich. 'Put your shoes on, you have to come with us, you can eat your sandwich on the way.'

We set off for the Manager's office which was a good few minutes' walk away and for some reason, we arranged ourselves one on each side and one at the back just in case he decided to run off. Actually, he showed no sign of this and walked along happily eating his food without an apparent care in the world.

We arrived at the general office and walked in to the anteroom which doubled as reception and the secretary's office. 'Morning, Mabel,' we all said in unison. I noticed with some disquiet a deputy head keeper's hat hanging on the peg. It wasn't mine, too clean, so guess who?

'So this is our mystery man,' said Mabel, so the word had got around, not surprisingly. 'I was expecting some wild creature with a bone through his nose. He seems quite tame.'

'That's a good one, Mabel.' (I don't think.)

You have to go straight in; he's waiting for you.

A short rap on the door. 'Come in,' a voice replied. We did, pushing the boy ahead of us.

'Good morning, all,' said Walt, 'I see you have managed to capture our trespasser. What have you to say for yourself, my lad?'

'Morning, Geoffrey,' said Joe, 'he's not uttered a word since we first met him so I don't think you are going to get an answer. Let me tell you what happened this morning.'

'Disgraceful, bloody vandal,' Spencer interjected. 'Just think of the reputation of the zoo, kidnapping, harm to the animals, harm to the public, everyone else coming in here stealing. We have rules. We need to call the police.'

I had forgotten about Spencer who had been sitting behind the door as we came in but had now almost literally exploded into life and was virtually jumping up and down in a frenzy. He had gone a strange shade of puce and a large strand of hair had escaped the Brylcream and was flopping around over one eye. We were hypnotised by the scene and it took some time for someone to break the tirade. The boy stood there with a quizzical expression on his face quite like the look and effect Moby usually had on me.

'Sit down, Spencer,' shouted Walt, 'and for God's sake, calm down. Nothing is going to be gained by getting hysterical. He seems quite well behaved so let's hear some ideas.'

'Let's lock him up just in case,' muttered Moby.

'I don't think that it is necessary,' said Joe, 'he seems harmless enough, and he has not tried to escape or behave badly.'

'Well, he escaped last night.'

'He was not locked up, Spencer, and he was in a safe place.'

'If you think that sleeping in a rough hut on an island with a load of wild gibbons, then I am a monkey's uncle,' screamed Moby.

Unfortunate turn of phrase, Moby, I thought. If it came to a choice, I would go with the monkey's uncle. This was a thought best kept to myself, so I just snorted.

'And you're just as bad,' he raged, 'you should have listened to me. I have been here longer than you.'

I assume this was a vague attempt at exerting his superiority but with his complexion running rampant, his hair a "flop" over one eye, the other staring like a madman and now a slaver of drool running down the side of his mouth, it was all I could do not to laugh. How I kept myself under control, I do not know. All I do know is that Molly didn't.

Quiet up to now. 'Bloody fool,' she said.

'Calm down, the lot of you!' shouted Walt. I could even hear Mabel giggling in the next office. Sober minds, sober thought.

I have to say at this point being sober was the last thing on my mind but when in front of your superiors, it is wiser to keep your mouth firmly shut.

'May I suggest something, Geoffrey? said Joe.

'Please do Joe, I hope it is something constructive,' he said, glaring at Moby.

51

'There is something very unusual going on here and I would like to get to the bottom of it. I have never seen animals behave in this way before and I would like to keep him here with us while we make some enquiries. He could help Ben out. That will keep him out of trouble. Molly has already made him up a bed. What do you think?'

'Ridiculous,' spat Moby, 'have you lost your mind? If he is going to be given the runabout of this place, I am going to carry a stick and keep my gun close. You never know, we could all be murdered in our beds.'

'Thank you, Spencer, I think you are getting hysterical, so just shut up. I have to say that I am also intrigued by this young man and your suggestion, Joe, is a good one. Ben, he's now your responsibility.'

'Clear off, you lot, thank you Joe, thank you Molly. No, I don't want to hear any more from you Spencer. Ben, wait and give me a minute.'

The four of them left and I could hear them talking to Mabel before the outside door closed.

'Keep him away from Spencer, Ben. I know what you think of him but he is a senior member of staff and you need to give him some respect as he has been here man and boy.'

'Mr Whitlam, I do try my hardest to get on with Spencer, but he is very trying. I have had very real thoughts of killing him several times and have dreamed of feeding his carcass to the warthogs.'

'Ben, that is not funny and I wonder if you need some therapy as well. Remember also that I would have to answer to my sister (his mother) and being cut up and fed to the pigs would be light relief compared to getting on the wrong side of her. My last word is that you have some flexibility, he does not, so the onus is on you.'

'I will do my best, Mr Whitlam.'

'I know you will.'

'After all, you and Spencer have a lot in common.'

Whaaat! Walt, are you on another planet, I thought, *I have absolutely nothing in common with Spencer, physically, emotionally or any other…ally for that matter. We work in the same place and we are both male and I'm not even sure whether Spencer fits that last one.*

On the way out of the office, to join the others who were waiting outside, I mused on how unfair life could be when I, a relatively normal human being, would have to give sway to a drooling imbecile who has about as much insight and charisma as a two-inch nail.

Luckily outside, there were only the three of them waiting, Spencer having sloped off to sulk, no doubt, in the undergrowth. Probably gone to oil, his gun and plot how to aggravate the situation in whatever way he could. It was going to be like walking on eggshells!

We headed off back to the restaurant and Molly disappeared in the back somewhere leaving us three to have a snack and plan what we were going to do.

'Right my lad,' said Joe, 'you listen to Ben here and he will tell you what you have to do. Here we go:

1. Do not go off alone.
2. Do not go into any of the enclosures unless Ben says it is OK.
3. Do not talk to any of the visitors, Oh! I forgot you don't speak to anyone anyway so scrub that one.

'Molly has made a bed up for you and I am now going to take a real chance. If you do not want to sleep in the room she has set aside for you, I will allow you to sleep on the island on four conditions:

'First, we have a camp bed which we will take over for you rather than sleeping on the straw.

'Second, you will use the little boat to go to and fro. I assume you have worked out how to use it. Remember to tie it up or you are going to go swimming.

'Third, if you sleep there, you will shower properly each morning and try and keep yourself reasonably tidy.

'Fourth and last, and this is from Molly, do not help yourself to food especially after you have been with the gibbons. If you want something to eat, ask Molly and we would prefer that you eat with one of us. If Ben has gone off duty and you want a late night snack, no doubt Molly will leave you something just in case.

'Now, do you agree to all this? I know you understand, so a nod will do.'

The boy nodded enthusiastically.

'Good,' said Joe, 'I'm off. Over to you, Ben, just keep him out of the way of you know who.'

We found the camp bed in one of the stores and it had obviously been left over from the war, as it was wooden-framed and khaki. Not sure which war however. It was not in the best of conditions, but it would do especially as it was destined for the main gibbon hut. We loaded some blankets and a water container and headed for the island.

'You can row over so I can see if you can handle it.'

Now rowing a boat for the first time is not easy. I have seen many people give up and use one oar as a paddle only to see them helplessly going around in circles. How those guys in coracles manage, I cannot imagine.

The problem is simple. You are sitting with your back to where you are going, then you have to make sure the oars are square in the water and you pull on them with the same amount of effort. If one oar is "under-squared" or not properly in the water at all, then you will fall backwards as there is no resistance.

After twenty minutes of experiencing all of the above and some near capsizes, we finally reached the far shore and he docked the boat with some effort.

'I think you have roughly got the hang of it,' I said, 'bring your things and you can put them inside the hut.'

While he was doing that, I was thinking. Does he realise that gibbons are inquisitive creatures. Yes, they have clearly accepted him but does he realise he is going to have several furry bedmates in there with him? There is always the room Molly prepared if it gets too much I suppose.

My last look at the hut was from the boat as we travelled back to the far shore and just as I expected there was a lot of gibbon activity in and around the main hut no doubt inspecting this new plaything.

'Now lad, instead of everyone wondering who you are, I am going to introduce you as a young student helper who is very shy so does not say much.'

Much, I thought, *he doesn't say anything!*

'I can't explain away your age as normally young volunteers have to be at least sixteen years, old so I will tell people that you just look young for your age. By the way, I can't keep calling you boy or lad so you must have a name. Do you have one? If you can't tell me, can you write it down?'

The boy slowly shook his head.

'OK. Plan B, we will have to think up a name. How do you feel about that?'

A shrug. *Mowglie would be good,* I thought.

I will sing out some names and you stop me if there is one you like.

After the usual John, Peter, Paul, names of the apostles' names of the Beatles, names from the Old Testament, names of Chelsea football players nothing seemed to hit the mark and I was running out of ideas and getting a bit desperate.

'How about Larry,' I said, 'it's like the Lar out of the Lar gibbons with a bit added to it.'

Now, this brought a response. He cupped his chin with one hand, looked at the island, then at me, smiled, yes smiled at last then nodded.

Larry it is then. I will get a badge made for you like everyone else, then it will stop you having to answer what your name is as you can just point to it. That is, unless you feel like speaking of course.

So off we went, at first with Larry walking alongside me, but soon "dragging his heels" as we passed each animal enclosure.

'Come on, keep up, Larry, we have work to do. Giraffes first.'

Giraffes are lovely graceful creatures and very calm unless you get near a female with a calf. Giraffes do not bite they trample and are known to kill big cats if the young are in danger. Other than this, the only strange sign of aggression are males who use their necks when rutting to claim superiority.

We had four giraffes. One male, two females and one calf. The calf was a great attraction for visitors and we were delighted when he was born, all legs and neck. He was five months old.

'This is James, who is a keeper as you can see. James, this is Larry who will be shadowing me to see how we do things around here.'

'Hello, Larry,' said James, 'welcome to the giraffes. Has Ben given you some information about them? With that, James started off on one of his pet subjects and Larry looked as he was in heaven. 'Are you a volunteer or a student? He looks a bit young, Ben.'

'Special case, James. You introduce Larry to your guys here.'

'Each keeper has a list of animals that they take special care of. One of James is the giraffes. So that makes James our giraffe expert. Let's help James with them, Larry,' I said, thinking to redirect his attention away from asking any more awkward questions.

'James will go in with the big male and the female as they know him and he will pull out the straw bedding to the edge where you will rake it by reaching through the bars. The old stuff goes into that pile over there and it will then be shredded and used on the gardens as fertiliser. Everything here is recycled where we can. If we cannot use it all, it is bagged up and sold to the local garden centre.

'While you are doing that, I will get some fresh branches and feed to give to James for them. One thing you will learn here is that everyone literally "mucks in". We all have to do the mucky jobs as well as the nice ones.'

The three giraffes have a large (and of course very tall) kind of warehouse building complete with two industrial roller shutter doors each one serving a separate fenced enclosure internally. Along the back, there are storage areas and on top of that a viewing gallery for the visitors. Their home is complete with a large paddock with public footpaths around two sides.

'When the baby was born,' James explained to Larry, 'the male giraffe was separated just to make sure the young one was not in danger. Baby giraffes tend to be a bit skittish and very wary of strangers or just about anything except their mother who stays very close by at all times.'

This is going well, I thought, *I quite like having him tagging along. He looks as though he will be useful. Wish he would speak but at least he looks calm and interested in everything.*

I went outside to get some freshly cut branches, leaving James inside the enclosure and young Larry patiently waiting for the soiled bedding to be pushed towards the inner fence.

I came back in dragging an over-large branch through the rear storage door.

'Ben, look at this,' said James. 'He's climbing on the fence and he's going to hurt himself in a minute. Look, he's going to frighten them.'

'Just wait a moment, James. He's not going to fall, he's as agile as a monkey, that one. He should come down though.'

'Well, I never, would you look at that,' exclaimed James, 'they're not scared of him at all, in fact, the mother seems to be pushing her calf towards him. Never seen that before. The mother normally gets between her calf and any sort of danger. Now, both the others are coming over. Better get him away. They won't bite but the adults may try to knock him off with their necks.'

'Just wait a minute, James, hand Larry up a new branch then let's step back a bit and see what happens.'

Giraffes have very large tongues which they wrap around branches or vegetation to pull them apart to mouth-sized bites. Both giraffes latched on to the branch Larry was holding and then slowly and very gently moved close up to the fence. Larry by now was on top of the fence with one leg over each side. *Good job we were the only ones there,* I thought.

As we watched the two giraffes, mouths full of twigs and leaves, reached out with their necks to touch the boy while he just balanced on that fence staring at them intently.

After what seemed an age, he slowly climbed down and turned to us.

He gestured at the personnel door.

'I think he actually wants to go in there,' I said.

'Not a good idea,' said James, 'I am the only keeper that goes in there with them and then only when I have to. Don't want to spook them as they could do a lot of damage to themselves especially the calf who is still very vulnerable.'

'Are all the outside doors closed, James?'

'Yes, I always close the main doors and those up on the gallery when I am in here,' he said.

'Not a word to anyone, James, your call, but I would like to see what happens. He has a way with animals and I would like to see how they react.'

'Put like that, so would I,' said James, 'I still can't get over their reaction to him. Usually, I am the only person who can get near them and I have not even touched their baby from the day it was born.'

'James, you stand by their gate and I will stand back here out of the way. In fact, I will go up on the gallery. Just wait a minute.'

James went to the personnel gate and opened it slightly then gestured to Larry to come forward. Larry did not need any second bidding and was up to and through the gate before you could blink.

'I can't see what's happening,' shouted James.

I could. The male giraffe had stood by the gate and blocking his view. From above, I could see quite clearly. Larry was standing in between mother and calf his right hand on the mother's shoulder and his left on the calf's back. All three were placid and looking right at him. Larry's mouth was moving but I could hear no sound.

'It's gone very quiet,' said James. It hadn't really, as it had not been noisy in the first place so this was just a nonsensical statement.

'It's more than OK, James, move away from the door to your right and you will get a better view.'

'Wow, never seen anything like that before,' said James repeating himself, 'almost looks like they are talking to each other. Wish I had a camera, actually, no I don't. This is too private besides I would lose my job if this got out.'

'Come on out, now, Larry,' I said, 'that's enough for today. We don't want to risk anyone seeing you in there. Come on, quickly.'

The one thing you can say about Larry. He does what he's told. I am really enjoying him being around. He has given me a whole new perspective.

Fateful words!

The next 20 minutes were taken up with the tasks we had ascribed to ourselves with James shovelling and Larry raking and me in my senior position, not doing too much. Every few minutes, James would lift his head, look at Larry, then at the giraffes and then gently shoo them away to the other side of the enclosure. I could see the furrowed brow showing his thought processes working and a look of puzzlement on his face.

'Right, we are off now, James, on to the penguins and the coypus. Thanks for your help and understanding. Please do not tell anyone about this. It is not as secret but there are some people who would make a fuss.'

'Don't worry, I'm the last person to say anything. Very strange, I can't get over this. How long is he here for?'

'Not sure, when I know, I will tell you.'

'Maybe you could bring him here again tomorrow about this time when it is quiet. I would like to see if this is a "one-off" or if there is something I could get to understand.'

'We'll see, I am sure that Larry would go for it,' I replied.

Larry and I walked down the long path that joins on to what is for all practical purposes the main thoroughfare through the zoo. We walked in silence, as there was still a stout refusal on Larry's part to say anything. Every now and then, I had got used to firing a sudden question at him to see if I could catch him off guard. Nothing worked and far from catching him off guard, he never really seemed to be on it in the first place.

Saying that, Larry was not like other kids of his age who would either be excitedly asking questions by the dozen or in some pre-pubescent stupor or just trying to run off.

I can only describe it that being with Larry was like being with a child in wonderland. His eyes darted from place to place, enclosure to enclosure, creature to creature. It may have been my imagination but it was almost like the ones we did pass; the bison, camel, zebra and deer seemed to stop what they were doing and in some cases, move closer to us.

'Here we are, Larry, the penguins. Two types. The big ones are Emperor penguins and the others are Humbolts. They live quite happily together in this big enclosure and I can see that they have been fed and cleaned out already, so we will move on. Over the next few days, I will introduce you to their keeper and the lovely job of mucking out penguins.'

Most of the penguins had been standing around doing little or nothing as is their want while the others were swimming around mainly on the surface. As we leaned over the wall, I noticed a change in their demeanour. The swimming around stopped and those few jumped out of the water and stood on the bank with the others who had become suddenly more alert. They all stared at Larry and the boy stared back. *This was not uncommon,* I thought, the penguins know me and here is a new face that comes along when there is no one else around.

I tried to believe this myself. *Very odd,* I thought.

'You hungry, Larry, I am. Luckily, we are heading back towards the restaurant and it's tea time. Before we go there, we will do a detour around the top island.'

I suspected that Larry knew his way around this place nearly as well as I did and in his case, mainly in the dark so I did not have to guide him or show him the way. He just walk-trotted along beside me apparently happy as can be.

I remember telling you about the upper island and the lemur colony that inhabits it. The island is accessed by two rope bridges and the lemurs are left to go where they choose to the usual delight of the visitors. There is a hut in the middle where the lemurs can get away from the visitors and plastic shields on the end of each bridge to stop them wandering too far.

Signs say "Do not feed the animals" and "Do not hold them or try to pick them up". These usually work although we have had a couple of incidents with visitors and one with other animals.

One of the visitor incidents involved a young girl who decided she wanted to cuddle one of them and would not take no for an answer. Apparently, did her mother only not help but actually encouraged the kid.

Having received the "brush-off" by the lemur, the child then tried to pull him toward her by its tail. Given all this, I would have tried to bite her. He succeeded. The furore that this caused was monumental and the zoo reluctantly agreed to have the guilty animal put down to appease the family.

We were not even sure which was the guilty party so a show trial was set up and the chosen male was quickly bundled into a carry cage and spirited away supposedly to be taken to the vet on a one-way ticket. The reality of course was that we had no intention of doing away with the creature. First, there was an identity issue and second, it was not his fault. Who could blame him? They did!

The second visitor incident involved a spotty adolescent youth who we all agreed should have been pushed back into the womb and kept there.

This child of Satan decided that it would be fun to try to pick up a lemur, throw it into the lake to see if it could swim. Now one of the reasons that the lemurs have an island home is that they do not like water either so when this young fool tried to push the lemur off the rope into the lake, it just held on more tightly. Then to make it worse, a now frightened lemur found himself being torn off the rope and he decided that he had had enough. This time, it was not a finger that got bitten but the kid's ear which is far more painful.

This time, the zoo held its ground and told the parents in no uncertain terms that it was going to sue them. Thankfully, to back this up, a number of tourists had caught the whole action on their mobile phone cameras so they did not have a leg to stand on. Despite this, the future of the lemur sanctuary and its public access was debated long and hard and the vote for its closure narrowly defeated.

The most amusing episode was the "Great Escape". Well, I thought it was funny.

Lemurs live in colonies or a kind of extended family. They gather for protection and if they do something, they do it together. This particular summer evening, one adventurous lemur managed to convince the rest of the pack that an evening stroll might be fun. They were located by a horrendous noise on top of the spider monkeys' enclosure where they were teasing the inmates or just showing off their freedom to the captives within. Either way, the retrieval process was very difficult. The enclosure was made of a strong mesh on light metal angle framework. It easily held the combined weight of the six spider monkeys inside who were trying to poke their long fingers through the roof mesh and the dozen or more lemurs who were being very annoying above them.

Sadly, the additional weight of the two keepers were never included in the equation and the roof collapsed enfolding the two keepers and one lemur who had failed to jump clear in a sort of mixed humanity ball. The roof then tore off the end supports freeing the spider monkeys except one who was institutionalised.

It is interesting how animals sometimes get on with each other. Lemurs are from Madagascar separated from the nearest monkey by many miles of inhospitable ocean. I wondered if there was some sort of genetic memory that linked both species or whether it was just the heady rush of freedom that catapulted their escape into a near disaster.

To cut a long story short, the mob finally fetched up on the outside enclosure of the chimps. Very luckily for them, the large adult chimps were inside with the outside door shut to give the juveniles a bit of peace and quiet to play unhindered by their seniors.

Despite a plethora of Planet of the Apes films, people still seem to view chimpanzees as nice cuddly friendly creatures who are as close to us humans as can be. In the main, the youngsters are, which is why they are invited to the Chimps Tea Parties. However, when they can get old, they can get very crabby and they have big teeth and can be very dangerous.

So after several hours, the mob, now tired and probably missing their home and more likely their food, gave up without too much effort on our part. The lemurs were put in their hut on the island; given some food and ordered to cool off. The spider monkeys were allotted a temporary cage and told to await the repair of their old one. The incumbent monkey was given his own dwelling in case the others picked on him for being a "party pooper".

End result:

One broken cage.

Four stitches to one keeper's arm where he fell through the mesh.

A tribe of lemurs who were so frightened by their freedom that they have never tried it again, to date anyway.

Five spider monkeys who would definitely do it again if given the chance and one less adventurous one who has been repatriated with the others but is still being picked on.

Several hours of bureaucratic autopsy including a consultation with an animal behaviourist who some of us believe had to research what a lemur was in the first place.

If you want variety, work in a zoo!

Back to the story.

True to form, one look at Larry and he was covered in a hairy throng. For the first time, I heard a sound from him. Giggling. *So, he has a voice of sorts,* I thought, *maybe he just feels he has nothing to say.*

Larry disengaged himself with some effort and got across the bridge to me. The lemurs crowded up against the plastic wall and made small hooting noises.

Larry and I arrived at the restaurant sometime around seven in the evening to find Joe and Molly seated at their table. I say "their table" as Joe and Molly usually sought out each other's company at meal times and had a favourite place where they could see but not be so easily observed. This time, I saw them first and walked in on them deep in conversation.

We got the usual 'hello, my luvvers, here you are, bet you're hungry'. We were. Well at least I was, hard to tell with Larry. 'Sit down, I've kept something for you.'

'Now what have you been up to,' said Joe, 'what have you been up to?'

Between mouthfuls, I gave them a rundown of the events of that afternoon and the surprises that I had experienced.

'Ben,' said Joe very seriously, 'you need to keep some of these thoughts to yourself.'

'Why,' said I, 'there are some amazing things going on which I do not even start to understand.'

'That's the problem, Ben, you are excited and fascinated but there are those who would be frightened by anything strange and cause trouble.'

'Are you talking about Moby?' I said.

'Not necessarily, there are worse out there, believe me.'

'Your puddings are here,' shouted Molly, breaking the silence, 'come and get them.' We collected the dishes of apple pie and custard and went back to join Joe who had already eaten. Molly joined us.

'Pass me a spoon, please Larry,' I said.

'Why do you call him Larry?' Molly asked. 'It's not his name.'

'You must know something that I don't, Molly. I gave him a lot of choices and that was the one he seemed to like.'

'It's not his name,' she repeated.

'Then what is?' I said.

'You would not understand, Ben, it's not really a name, it's more a sound.'

'That's enough, Molly. You are talking too much and we do not know for sure,' said Joe sternly.

'What's going on, you two, and what on earth are you talking about, what do you know?'

'He's a special child, one of the old people,' Molly whispered.

'For God's sake, shut up Molly, we agreed you would not say anything until we knew more. Get away with you,' he snapped.

Molly left in a flood of tears obviously not having been spoken to by Joe like that before. Larry went with her.

'What's all this, Joe? You have to tell me now.'

'Ben, first of all you have to understand that Molly comes from the Moor and they have old ways and beliefs. I, too come from within that area. Old ways, old superstitions, old beliefs. Molly has the sight. She sees things that the rest of us can't or won't see. Don't take any notice. She has become fond of the boy and is only being protective.'

'Now you have really got me intrigued. I have heard some of the stories and you forget that I was brought up in these parts as well though not on the moor. Are you going to tell me or not?'

The tannoy came to life: It was Mabel still in the main office:

"WILL JOE AND BEN COME TO THE OFFICE IMME-DIATELY AND BRING THE BOY WITH YOU" it blared. Strange, no call on the mobiles, no please, better go quick.

The three of us cantered up to the main office. Molly followed though not invited. 'You had better wait outside,' said Joe.

'I'll sit in the office with Mabel,' said Molly. Mabel was looking anxious. Trouble was brewing or by the look of things had well and truly brewed.

'If that is you three come in,' said a voice clearly Walt's.

We did. Inside, Walt was sitting behind his desk and beside him a triumphant looking Spencer. To Walt's left and next to Spencer sat a woman whom at first glance looked like a sort of female version of Spencer. Black, lank hair, pointy nose, thin lips and a piercing gaze over a pair of narrow spectacles over which she peered in a less than friendly manner.

Next to her sat a police sergeant whom I recognised, as he and his family were regular visitors to the zoo.

'Hello, Reg,' I said, 'how are you?'

'Well,' he replied, 'but I am afraid it's Sergeant Reynolds to you today. I am on official business.'

'Sounds like I'm in trouble,' I joked.

'You could well be, kidnapping is serious.' Sergeant Reg was obviously not relishing his task here.

I am not good in these sort of situations, not that I have really been in one before so I started by pretending ignorance.

'Who's been kidnapped?' I asked.

'This is Miss Hoare from social services and they have been alerted to the fact that we have a young man here who is being kept against his will and that we are all apparently complicit,' said Walt. 'The sergeant is here to enforce the situation if need be.'

Before I proceed further, and to stop you readers tittering, I have to point out that Hoare is a very common name in these parts and there it ends as the Miss Hoare in front of me is the furthest thing from any "lady of the night" you might have come across.

There could be a tactic here, I thought, *to get on the right side of Miss Hoare.*

'How do you do Miss Hoare, my name is Ben, what should we call you?'

'I know who you are and what you are doing. My name is Ms, not Miss Hoare.' *Looks like she doesn't have a right side,* I thought. *Better keep my mouth shut with this one.*

'For a start,' exclaimed Joe, 'we have not and are not kidnapping anyone. We are looking after this young man as our guest. He is being housed, clothed and fed while we make enquiries as to where he comes from. In the meantime, he is helping out in the zoo.'

'He is a minor,' snapped Miss (sorry Ms) Hoare, 'this is not a proper home, he should not be working as he is under age and you are not qualified or fit to say what is best for him. We are also in the best position to find his family or where he came from.'

'We have plenty of junior volunteers here and the boy is happy where he is. Who are you to say different,' argued Joe. I joined in.

'It's my job,' shouted the woman above the din. 'We are taking him into care. We have to do this whether you like it or not. It is procedure when an official complaint has been made.'

'No one here has made a complaint, official or otherwise,' said an exasperated Joe. 'What's all the fuss about? No harm done.'

Walt looked embarrassed and turned his head to a triumphant Spencer.

'Fuck you, Moby,' I said.

Chapter 5
The Great Escape

We watched as Sergeant Reg took Larry by the arm and led him out of the office preceded by Ms Hoare. A wail went up from Molly in the outer room when she realised that the boy was being taken away. He had no expression and went meekly. Only when they reached the car did he glance back and gave a small wave.

To say Molly was distraught was an understatement. 'They don't realise what they are doing, he needs to be here where he is safe, with us, with the animals, do something, Joe.'

'I know how you feel, Molly, but we must keep clear heads. These people do not and will not understand and you might make things worse.'

'I need to talk to you two back in here,' shouted Walt, 'you better come in as well, Molly. Spencer, stay where you are, where I can see you. Make sure for the next twenty minutes you are just outside of my reach, my lad, as I have some words for you.'

We sat down facing Walt whose skin colour was beginning to return to something rather more normal and human.

'Look, I know you meant well, but this could be real trouble for the zoo and for us personally. As for you, Spencer, what the hell do you think you were playing at, you idiot. You just couldn't help yourself, could you?'

'I care about the zoo,' replied Spencer.

'You care about yourself, you mean. Damn fool thing to do. You put us all in the hot seat,' Walt exclaimed.

I could see that Walt was not getting through to Spencer and he still believed he had done no wrong. His eyes were beginning to moisten with righteous indignation. 'Rules are not to be broken,' he muttered.

'Shut up,' snapped Walt.

'Of all the stupid things—'

Walt cut me off. 'I'll do the talking, if you don't mind and even if you do. Get out all of you. I have got some thinking to do to work out some damage limitation. I can see the look on the Trustees' faces now. Oh God! What happens if the press get hold of this?'

We shuffled outside past the wide-eyed Mabel who had clearly been listening to every word. 'Poor lad,' she said quietly.

'Bloody trouble,' replied Spencer.

'Shut up, Moby,' I said angrily, without thinking.

Outside, I think all three of us had visions of wresting Moby to the ground and throttling the life out of him. Frankly, it would have been a service to humanity.

'Who's Moby?' said Moby.

'You are,' I said.

'Why?' he asked, puzzled.

'You work it out, give you something useful to think about,' said Molly.

Spencer strode off in his usual dogged fashion while we three repaired to our dining table.

'Any ideas?' said Molly. 'We can't just let them get away with this.'

'As I see it, we do not have much choice,' said Joe, 'they have the law on their side, so I cannot see what we can do. He's not a relative, we don't even know his name or where he comes from.'

'But he's special,' said Molly, trying to suppress more tears, 'maybe we could adopt him. Perhaps it's like the "lost and found", if no one claims him within a certain period then maybe we could claim him like they do at the RSPCA.'

'Nice thought, Molly,' I said, 'but I don't think it quite works like that with children. Besides none of us is in a position to adopt a child, we would have to prove that we had a stable home. I'm not married, Joe's a widower and Molly, you live alone as well.'

'Well—' Molly began.

'You are right, Ben,' said Joe, interrupting and glaring at Molly, 'we will have to come at this problem another way.

'I have had enough for today. Home time, I think and we will see what tomorrow brings.'

Eight o'clock the following morning, Joe and I were sitting gloomily at the same table. Molly was hovering with a huge teapot in her hand. By the state of her eyes, she had clearly been crying most of the night.

'WILL JOE, SPENCER AND BEN COME TO THE OFFICE, PLEASE,' Mabel on the loudspeaker system. At least we got a please this time!

Joe and I quickly walked to the main administration building and were shown in to Walt's office by Mabel. Molly had again followed but stopped and sat down in a chair in the corner of Mabel's office. We were surprised to see Ms Hoare sitting in front of Walt plus Spencer who managed to get there somehow before us.

'It is our usual procedure,' began Miss Hoare, 'for a member of our staff to report back to the people involved in this matter as quickly as possible to put their minds at rest. I can tell you that the boy has been accommodated in the children's home not far from here.

He is at present undergoing a medical examination after which he will be further questioned after which we will try to find out where he comes from. The police tell me that there is no report of any missing child matching his description so they are extending their enquiries further afield in case he comes from another part of the country.

'But what—' I said.

'Please let me finish without further interruption,' she said primly.

'So far, the boy has shown no inclination to answer any of the questions put to him. He is not amenable to instruction and has refused to eat but it is early days and we believe that this situation will improve once he becomes more familiar with his new surroundings.'

This sounds like one of our speeches when we introduce a new animal, I thought. *This one's a cold fish and no mistake.*

Ms Hoare then commenced a long diatribe about the official procedures "to put our minds at rest!" and mine in the meantime started wandering.

I looked across the room at Spencer who was unusually silent and he was just staring wide-eyed at her (well as wide-eyed as his squinty ones would go). A look of almost rapture on his face and suddenly, I realised that to him, Ms Marjorie (yes, that's her name) Hoare was a thing of rare beauty and he was besotted and doting on her every word and gesture.

Now they say that beauty is in the eye of the beholder but this was pushing the boundaries off that one a long way out.

'Now in conclusion,' said Ms Hoare, 'it is not practical for me to report to everyone here on our progress with the boy so I would ask you to elect one person with whom I can liaise.'

Spencer's hand shot up like he was in first grade kindergarten. 'I would like to volunteer,' he cried.

'Well, we do like a bit of enthusiasm,' she said. 'I will put your name on my form. I have Mr Whitlam's details down as the person in charge and I have your two names,' peering at Joe and me over her glasses, 'from Sergeant Reynolds, so what is yours.'

'Spencer Wilks, spelt S P E N C E R then W I L K S,' he stuttered, 'would you like my address and home telephone number, Miss Hoare, I mean Marjorie. Can I call you Marjorie…please?'

'Thank you, Mr Wilks—'

'No, call me Spencer.'

'No, Mr Wilks will do fine, thank you, but I can contact you here if I need to.'

'But I have all sorts of information to add,' he pleaded.

'Shut up, Spencer,' said Walt.

'Yes, shut up, Spencer,' said Joe, 'you have done enough damage already.'

'I've not seen such crawling since I watched the tarantulas last, Moby,' I said.

'You are not helping either,' said Walt.

'Who's Moby?' asked Ms Hoare.

'Spencer.'

'Out of interest, why do you call him Moby?' she inquired.

''Cos he's a dick,' I said.

'I don't get it.' She looked quizzical.

If Moby has anything to do with it, you never will, I thought.

The next two days passed without incident apart from second hand reports from Mabel via Spencer Ms Hoare had paid another visit and had reported that the boy was not cooperating and it would appear had become quite a handful. Mabel heard Spencer say that he was not surprised and that the boy was probably a dangerous lunatic that had escaped from somewhere.

Next mealtime, we had another of our "worry" meetings.

'How about if we suggest we go and see him and take one of the animals with us. Maybe one of the young gibbons or Jacob the lone spider monkey or even a penguin. He liked the penguins,' I said.

He liked all the animals and I don't fancy a car ride with a Humbolt penguin shitting on my lap all the way. You know what they do when they are scared or parted from the others. Crap,' replied Joe.

'Well, let's see what the others think.'

The idea was presented to Walt who then relayed it on to Spencer. This, then, lead to a visit to us from Spencer at the following mealtime.

'Hello, Spencer,' said Molly, 'can I bring you something to eat?' Joe and I looked at each other and then at Molly, as there was something in the sweetness of her tone that rang danger signals in our minds.

'I expect Spencer has already eaten, Molly,' said Joe.

'Oh, I think a busy man like Spencer can always do with a little something extra,' she said, with a hint of menace.

As usual, it had all gone straight over Spencer's head and the fact that we were trying to protect him from an overdose of rat poison and a twelve-year stretch for us for aiding and abetting.

'No, but thanks anyway,' he said, 'but I have been thinking about your idea of taking an animal to see the boy. Great idea as long as it is docile and cuddly. Marjorie would love it.'

It's Marjorie now, is it? I thought, and my imagination took a turn for the worse with visions of the two of them coupled together, peering lovingly and myopically at each other while spearing each other with their pointy noses. Have you ever seen an Aye-Aye? Look it up. We don't have any at the zoo but they are the ugliest animal you could imagine. They must have some sort of feral attraction and reproduce otherwise there would not be any left.

So maybe there is hope for Spencer and Marjorie after all. Yuk!

'So, I suppose that you would be the one to take the animal to her,' said Joe.

'Of course,' he replied, 'after all, I am the designated contact.'

'How about one of the African porcupines,' said Molly, 'you could hold it on your lap while you drive.'

'I don't think she would like one of them,' said Spencer, missing the very obvious sarcasm, 'she would prefer something cuddly.'

'Forget about taking an animal, just go yourself,' I said, 'I'm sure she would like to cuddle you, Spencer.' Muffled guffaws in the background.

His expression took on a dreamy look. Well as dreamy as any expression could look on his face. 'Do you really think so?'

'Absolutely Spencer, don't mess about, take her in your arms and just go for it,' I said.

'What do you mean, go for it?'

'The big smacker straight on the lips. We can all see she likes you so it's not time to be feint-hearted. Be brave, be a man, go get your woman, Spencer.'

73

Now all this time I am trying to put on concerned expression while in the background the other two are now crouched behind the servery counter stuffing tea towels in their mouths.

'What do you think, Molly?' he asked. 'You're a woman.' Joe and Molly had to recover very fast and started cleaning non-existent cutlery with the tea towels.

'Well, my luvver, Ben's right, you just get over there and get stuck in.'

'I'll do it,' he said, jumping to his feet, ignorant of the fact that I had just saved him from a certain unpleasant death and us out after eight years with good behaviour.

Spencer left in a hurry clearly filled with a new purpose.

'I would love to be a fly on the wall,' I said, laughing. Joe and Molly had reverted back to the tea towels, as Freddy had just walked in.

'What's so funny?' he asked.

'Can't tell you, Freddy, but Spencer is almost certain to lose one or both of his testicles sometime this afternoon.'

'Didn't know he had any,' said Freddy.

It was not until the following day until we came across Spencer who was secretly writing something on a clipboard on his lap.

'What are you up to, Spencer?' I asked.

'Nothing,' he replied, shielding the paper with his arm, 'none of your business.'

'How was the lad?'

'Didn't see him, he was locked up. Been violent to one of the staff there. Told you he was dangerous.'

'Good things though. Taking Marjorie out tonight. You were right. Thanks for the advice.'

'You actually kissed her?'

'Well, not exactly, but I did ask her out.'

My mind works in peculiar ways and a sudden surge of guilt came over me. I could be responsible for propagating a species. A new order. Little Spencers and Marjories. What have I done? I could plead insanity, I could blame the medication. Help!

Back to reality.

'So you are none the wiser about the boy. Nothing to tell us.'

'Only that by the time I left, he was sitting quietly in the sun room and according to the lady there, he had calmed down and was eating properly so they had no reason to lock him up again.'

The following day was a day to remember indeed. About three in the afternoon, my mobile rang. We used these in and around the zoo as intercoms especially when and if the call was of a private nature and we didn't want anyone to hear. 'See message,' said Mabel quickly.

Message ran "GO TO BABOONS URGENT".

I went to the baboons urgently.

It only took me a few minutes to get to the baboon enclosure and there were already a large crowd of people there. As I approached, I recognised Sergeant Reynolds mainly because he is large and was in uniform plus another younger constable. Next to them was the redoubtable Marjorie complete with Spencer at her side and another woman I didn't recognise.

On top of the wall was Matt who is the keeper in charge of the baboons.

Let me break off here for a minute to give you some background.

Although we don't have a real hierarchy, Matt comes under and reports to Spencer. Well comes under and reports is a bit of an exaggeration as Matt is what we call "unusual".

Matt is tall and lanky probably about six feet three (195 centimetres for you metric types). He has dreadlocks and would have been at Woodstock if he hadn't been born too late. He wears zoo trousers but to Spencer's absolute disgusts, insists on wearing a tie and die t-shirt. Once Spencer told him to take it off. He did and scared some of the visiting children with his tattoos.

Now whether by accident or design, Matt gets to look after all the animals that others do not want. The strange thing is that he doesn't seem to mind but sort of considers it as a badge of honour. Mind you, I have caught him smoking some interesting home-grown substances behind the rhino enclo-sure. No wonder they are docile.

He has the two camels one of them is particularly mean and bites. Both spit and are cantankerous.

The six zebra. They say that no one has ever been able to tame a zebra. Matt would agree.

The two warthogs. Ugly beasts with sharp tusks. They will run at or past you and slit you open so beware.

The two African porcupines. Now I like these two, but you have to watch them if they turn around on you. They are able to stick their back quills into a concrete wall and we have had to rescue a couple of guys who were cornered in their pen try-ing to retrieve some quills which are much prized as fishing floats. I have two myself. However, the quills have an irritant and wounds can quickly become infected. Worse, they have a small barb on the end so you have to push them out rather than pull them. Ouch!

Matt, himself, nearly lost his left leg from getting a quill through his calf and had several weeks off work, two of them in hospital.

And finally, the baboons.

Baboons live in colonies. We have about forty of them as they breed and adapt very easily. They have a strict hierarchy and are very dangerous. The problem with them is that unlike a pair of other animals, there are more of them, they know how to hunt as a pack; they have big teeth and they are very unpredictable. Personally, I think they are more trouble than they are worth but the visitors love watching their antics.

The baboons live in a large sunken compound which is some ten feet below the surrounding ground level. The perim-eter is further secured by a three-foot wall. In the middle of the compound is Baboon Mountain, an artificial concrete structure with shallow and deep caves. Going into the baboon enclosure is akin to a military operation and not something I relish but there are times when we have to rescue one of them if ill or wounded or for cleaning or maintenance.

Today was different.

There huddled in one of the shallower niches about two thirds up the twenty-foot "mountain" was Larry. He seemed none the worse for wear and sitting next to him was one of the big alpha males with absolutely no sign of their habitual aggression.

I walked around the path towards the two policemen. 'What's going on?' I asked.

'Pretty bloody obvious,' said Sergeant Reg. Kid fooled the staff, did a runner, fetched up here and won't come out.'

'No good shouting at him,' I said, 'it will just scare him more and you might set off the baboons. They can get hysterical and start attacking people so best to stay calm.'

'Thank you, David Attenborough,' said Reg, 'what do you suggest?'

'No need for sarcasm, Sergeant, if you had left well enough alone this would not have happened,' I replied. *Get that dig in,* I thought, though my timing could have been better.

'Spencer, this is your territory, why don't you go in and get him out. Take Marjorie to help you,' I shouted to him.

'Very funny,' he replied, 'my answer would not be suitable for a lady's ears.'

I looked around theatrically for a lady. There was only Marjorie and the other unknown female and neither would have made the centrefold of Gardening Weekly.

Joe had now appeared and quickly followed by Molly who had no doubt been alerted by her confidante Mabel.

'Right Sergeant,' he said, 'I have six more keepers on their way with all the paraphernalia then there are the four of us here as well including Spencer. If you would gently and very quietly move the crowd down the hill, two of our lads will cordon off the path. Spencer, you look after the two ladies and keep them well out of the way.

'Now we are going to have two teams of three with nets to crowd the baboons into the corner away from the mountain. Some are going to get by so there will be two keeper to try and keep them off with sticks.

'Once we have got most of them past the mountain, then Ben here can do his alpine bit and go and grab the boy.'

'I'll go too,' said Molly, 'he knows me.'

'Well, the baboons don't, so no chance. Spencer, here's another one for you to look after. I am relying on you. Do not let me down or you will be on permanent baboon duty.'

The policemen did their bit and the mob moved away albeit reluctantly. The cordons went up and as I was putting on my Kevlar neck guard (baboons like biting necks) and heavy gloves, I noticed Spencer leading Marjorie away with his arm around her waist and… Marjorie was not putting up any resistance.

I blame myself but this is not the time.

Two ladders were fetched and the two teams went into action. It looked a bit like native fishing without the water.

The baboons were having a great time. Catch me if you can; practising body swerves to dodge the netters, it was baboon heaven. Made a nicer changer from picking body lice off each other or watching to see who might be trying to interfere with your woman.

Spencer, I thought, *you are never going to have that problem. Not sure about the lice though.*

'Right,' shouted Joe, my signal, down the ladder, across the enclosure and up the mountain. I went up and sat next to Larry who did not move. 'Hi Larry, nice to have you back. Who's your friend?' I said looking at the large male sitting next to him that refused to be herded away.

The baboon showed his teeth at me which is definitely not a good sign but Larry just took his hand and stroked the back of it and the baboon's face went into a kind of repose.

'Come on down with me, Larry, you can't stay here. If you don't, the keepers will use the dart gun on the animals and that can be dangerous to them if they get too much dosage especially the little ones. So say cheerio to your pal there and follow me.'

Larry stroked the face of the baboon and touched his forehead with his own then shuffled on his bottom down the concrete crags to the enclosure floor then up the ladder. The baboon just sat there quietly and the keeper teams reversed out of the enclosure leaving the baboons to no doubt ponder on what might have been.

'You come along with me,' said a voice that I recognised as Sergeant Reg, 'you have some explaining to do.'

'For goodness sake Sergeant, can't you just back off,' said Molly, who had appeared at the parapet, 'it didn't work last time and it isn't going to work now, so you would be better off leaving this to us. Besides, I don't know what you think he is going to explain, as he hasn't opened his mouth once yet.'

'I'm only doing my duty, Ma'am.' *That old stock phrase,* I thought. 'You have to remember it is not my decision.'

'No,' said Ms Hoare, 'it's mine and he's going back where he came from and this time he is not going to escape, will he?' she said looking at the other woman. 'By the way, I haven't introduced you, this is Ms Cartwright who runs the children's home.'

'How do you do?' I said. 'Is there a Mr Cartwright?'
Don't you love these rhetorical questions?

The answer I got was not voiced but her look could have peeled paint off the walls. My guess it was a no. Not surprised! I had very unpleasant visions of Spencer, Marjorie and Ms Cartwright coupled in some unholy threesome but I have to admit that there is something wrong with my mind sometimes and thankfully, that vision evaporated from my mind as quickly as it had appeared.

So off they went again, Sergeant Reg with his grip on Larry's arm followed by his constable, the two women and of course Spencer.

The keepers had disappeared all but Matt who was studying his charges for signs of distress. Molly was again in tears being comforted by Joe. Mabel had appeared no doubt to report back to Walt, the man himself being absent as usual.

You know something, I thought, *we haven't seen the end of this.* I was dead right.

Chapter 6
A Plan is Formed

The three of us felt very down about Larry being taken away for a second time but life in the zoo had to go on, so the next few days slipped by without any great incident except for King, the male lion, who had got a growth on his foot which was getting bigger by the day. Daniel, his keeper, was worried. His name's not Daniel really, it's Ken, but we call him that because he looks after the lions and other big cats so he is "Daniel from the lion's den". No prizes for originality.

I went by at his request and there he was in deep conversation with James. They were planning how to go about getting a biopsy which is no easy matter. King has to be separated, then drugged with just the right amount of sedative. Too much and it can cause heart failure, too little and you could end up with one angry lion waking up with you in a very confined space. To make matters worse, the protocol is that there must be no exit left open in case the roused animal makes a bid for freedom and mauls a visitor. Keepers are expendable you see in terms of liability but quite low down the food chain in terms of menu.

So, on this occasion, King was bribed to go into a solitary cage with a rather nice looking piece of brisket. Then the sensible thing would be to sedate him with the dart gun. Unfortunately, Daniel decided that it would be less traumatic to his precious charge if he were injected by hypodermic.

The next twenty minutes would have been laughable had it not been so downright dangerous. First, King, faced with humans in fairly close proximity did the usual lion thing and faced the potential danger snarling, in a crouch with his bum the furthest part away possible.

Next, the hypodermic was being wielded by a junior keeper whose nervousness was being transmitted to the animal who was getting more irate by the minute.

'Daniel, I'll fetch the gun,' I said.

'No,' he replied, 'I've got this, just pull back a bit away from the cage.'

'It's been twenty minutes, the creature is getting worse and you and your pal here are no nearer getting it done.'

We pulled back and the lion started to calm down finally coming to rest in a perfect position against the bars with his back to us.

What happened next happened very quickly. Junior keeper moves forward, syringe in hand and instead of sticking it, straight in decides to give the target area a wipe with an alcohol swab.

There is a time and a place, and this was not it. King jumped up with impressive speed and the keeper had not quite withdrawn his hand when he struck.

I went to get the gun.

So half an hour later, we have King, the lion, out for the count with tongue lolling nicely out of his mouth and Daniel sitting next to him stethoscope in hand to keep check on the heartbeat. James was excising the growth which he said looked like a benign tumour but that the biopsy would be conclusive on that one.

The junior keeper called Rob sat nursing his hand which was bleeding copiously. 'You need some stitches in that, Rob,' I said. Rob was looking pale either from what had been or what was to come or both.

'Take him to the hospital then,' said James through he sutures he was holding in his mouth.

'Thought you could sort him out, you have all the stuff here.'

'I'm a bloody vet not a doctor, I could get struck off.'

'We're not going to tell and I don't think you can get struck off anyway for that.'

'Oh, all right, just let me finish these last two stitches.'

After few minutes of shrieking from Rob and the threat of me giving him the business end of the dart gun, his hand was done.

'Now for the tricky part,' said James, now sutureless, got to protect the wound from getting infected. Bandages are no good. He will have them off in a minute, so I am going to use the medical film.'

The film is a kind of shrink-wrap cling film. Very high tech and allows the wound to breathe but keeps germs out. It also has the advantage of being very flexible like a second skin so less likely to irritate and be then chewed off.

'Right, let's get him back in the carry cage before he wakes up,' said James, 'gently roll him over on to the stretcher.'

'You had better be quick,' interrupted Daniel, 'I think he's coming to.'

So we got King onto the stretcher and then the procedure was to bring the cage to the door. Then both sliding vertical cage doors would be clipped in the open position. Four of us would then pick up the stretcher and walk into the cage.

This was the tricky bit as if the lion decided to wake up, there would be two people between him and freedom and I would defy anyone in that situation to stick to protocol and allow themselves nobly to be eaten to save some visitor from a grisly death.

As senior, I decide to be on the front end of the stretcher with James leaving Daniel and Rob at the rear. It looked like a safer plan, for us two anyway.

The process went smoothly, the stretcher was lowered to the cage floor, James and I hopped out and secured one cage door. The other two did likewise the other end, and there he was safe and sound.

The final stage was to wheel the cage, now covered, back to the lion enclosure where King would have to recuperate on his own in the smaller cage. The cage was duly offered up and chained to the enclosure cage and the door lifted.

The signs of waking up had been wrongly interpreted and it was probably him dreaming of hunting antelopes. He was well under and now comfortable again, had started snoring.

'It's taking a long time,' said James, after sitting there for a good half hour, 'should have woken up by now.'

'Give him a prod,' I said, 'looks like he's just asleep.'

Daniel reached into the cage and shook the lion on his rump. No reaction. 'How much did you give him, Rob?'

'Well, I gave him the dose you said but added another 10ccs just to make sure,' said Daniel, still holding his injured hand, 'I was told that working out the dosage by animal weight is not always fool proof, so I thought it would be a good idea especially after his reaction to me.'

'You idiot, it's not your job to think, too much book learning, you could have killed him,' shouted Daniel, 'you can stay here with him until he wakes up. Don't touch him, just sit there and then call me when he comes around.'

'I have to go home soon,' Rob muttered moodily.

'You stay there, sunshine, until I say so. You are lucky you are going to have a job to come back to tomorrow.'

'Very important that King is not allowed back in with the two females,' said Daniel, 'funny thing about animals, but they sense injury or weakness and will pick on him until he fully recovers.'

It was now getting late and we carried equipment back to the surgery and the gun back to its case in the store next door.

'Right, I'm off for a final round before I knock off,' I said.

'I'm going to check on Rob and King,' said Daniel.

'I'm going home,' said James.

We are creatures of habit, and I am no exception so I took my usual circular route, first around the perimeter enclosures and then to the central ones finally ending up at the restaurant. I sat outside for a moment taking in the peace and quiet as a fond farewell to that day.

I looked across at Gibbon Island and pondered anew on the events of the last few weeks.

Hang on a minute, where's the boat? I thought. It's not tied up to the dock. I got up and walked toward the lakeside to see if it had slipped away or even sunk but there was no sign. I then started walking clockwise around the lake and very soon, I saw the yellow hull of the little boat pulled up on the far side of the island.

What on earth, it could not have drifted and hauled itself up. There was only one explanation.

Larry had escaped again and he was back. Excited, I decided I had to go and tell Joe before the hue and cry started all over again.

I think I mentioned that the zoo was built in a valley and at the top, there was a rear gate through which the public were not allowed. On the other side were playing fields, then a thirty-something year old housing estate of small neat bungalows. Joe lived in one of these.

I was over the gate and running across the field in a matter of minutes. I knew which bungalow was his but in all the sixteen years I had known him, I had never been in his home. When we socialised, it was always somewhere else so it had not dawned on me until then.

I opened the small garden gate and walked up to a neatly painted front door and rapped on it.

Sound of footsteps and Joe appeared at the door wearing his zoo trousers and just a vest.

'Joe,' I gasped breathlessly, 'he's back, Larry's back, he's on the island, he must have escaped, they'll find him—'

'Slow down, Ben, did you see him, how do you know for sure?'

'The boat was gone and pulled up on the far side of the island. Who else would do that?'

'What's all the noise,' called a voice, Molly's voice, 'there's a lot of excitement going on out there.'

'I'm glad you're here as well, Molly.' I stalled for a moment. 'Errr, why are you here?'

'You had better come in, my lad. Now you have found us out, time to come clean.'

I was ushered into the sitting room and there was Molly. 'Come in my luvver and welcome.'

'Well, it is a nice coincidence that you are here as well, Molly, because I think that Larry has escaped and is back on the island.'

'Two things,' said Molly. 'First, I am not surprised, that young man is special and I was expecting him. This is probably the first real place he has ever had where he feels safe and at home. Second about this so-called coincidence—'

'Molly,' Joe said sharply.

'It's no good, Joe, we've hidden this for so long and it's nothing to be ashamed of so it's good to tell someone like Ben who we trust.'

'OK, I suppose so, but not a word to anyone else,' said Joe quietly.

'Oh, I see, typical man,' laughed Molly, 'it's all right to live together but not all right to tell anyone. Anybody would think you were ashamed of me and us.'

'You're right, of course, as usual, Molly, I give in.'

'I like a man to know when he's beaten,' giggled Molly.

'I lost my wife about two years before you joined the zoo. She had been ill for a long time and finally slipped away. We had been married fifteen years, no children although we tried. Molly and I have always been friends from the first time we met, although it was at that time, platonic, as you say. Molly was and still is my rock. She helped me get through that awful time in my life and our friendship just naturally expanded into love. Just over ten years ago, we decided that we should live together. Saves on heating,' he joked.

'My story is a bit different, as I never married and spent many years looking after my father after mum died,' she said, 'met Joe, fell for him even when he was married and waited for my time. Long wait, but here we are. Joe is going to marry me one day. Make an honest woman of me.'

'Don't hold your breath, woman.'

'It's just taking you a bit longer to realise you are well and truly hooked.'

'Now I have got over my initial surprise, I have got to tell you that I am so pleased. You are my two most favourite people in the world. Should I say congratulations, perhaps not, seems a bit crass after all this time. Wow, I don't really know what else to say.'

Funny, but now I think on this, many things seem to fall into place and I am a bit surprised that I had never put two and two together before. The signs were all there to see but as my Grandma used to say, 'There's none as blind as them that won't see.'

'Back to the problem in hand,' said Joe, 'do we tell Walt because if we don't, someone else will and then Spencer will bludgeon into it all over. Then we have to consider aiding and abetting a runaway. Might be a crime for all I know. I have an idea that Sergeant Reg might want a nice juicy kidnapping on his books to break the tedium of his normal existence. We are going to have to be very careful. Let's give it some thought and talk about some options before we do anything else.'

'Do you have to be anywhere, Ben?' said Molly.

'No, I just have the two bedroom flat by the harbour, one cat, one motorbike that's all.'

''Bout time you found a young lady, Ben. You're good looking lad, you must have had girlfriends.'

'Had a few, but the longest was about eight months then we sort of drifted apart.'

'Well, time is passing by,' said Molly, 'you need to stay on your toes in case the right one turns up.'

Strange, when I think back on that conversation and what was in stall for me. Maybe she had the "second sight" after all.

A few drinks later and we were not really any further forward, so we decided to get some rest and tackle it afresh in the morning.

Short of sleep and a bit puffy-eyed, I got up the following morning and looked out of the window. Nice day, think I will take the motorbike, blow away some cobwebs. I was "tootling" along on my 400cc Honda four which in normal speak means going at about 40 mph, when a police van screamed past me with siren blaring followed by two unmarked cars travelling, I thought, *way too fast.*

'Where's the fire,' I said to myself, they were heading out of town, turned left about half a mile in front of me and then disappeared. As I approached their turning, I realised it was also my turning and a pit started forming in my stomach. They were heading for the zoo.

Fearing the worst, I did something I do not usually do and drove through the main gate that had been opened for them and headed for Walt's office. Sure enough parked outside were the police van and the two unmarked cars except as I got nearer, I could see that one of them had small markings denoting that it belonged to the local council social services.

I went inside the main office reception and there was Mabel trying to deal with a throng. Sergeant Reg, two constables, Ms Cartwright, another lady and, of course, the redoubtable Marjorie Hoare.

'Mr Whitlam is on his way here,' shouted Mabel above the din, 'you will have to be patient, he only lives just down the road, he's coming.'

Sergeant Reg spotted me in the doorway. 'You stay right there,' he commanded, 'bet you're mixed up in this somehow.'

'Mixed up in what exactly,' I replied.

Ms Cartwright broke in. 'The boy attacked a member of staff, broke two windows and escaped. We think he will have headed this way.'

'When was this?' I asked.

'Night before last,' said a constable.

'If he escaped the night before last, then why are you only here now? If you are right, he would have made his way straight here.'

'We had a report from that a boy of that description was seen heading north form the children's home in the opposite direction to here,' the constable said.

'Now, constable, don't be giving him too much information, he's probably involved in this,' said the sergeant.

'Well,' I said truthfully, 'I can honestly say that I have not seen him.'

With that, a flustered Walt arrived. 'What's going on? What are you lot doing in my office?'

Sergeant Reg produced a black flip-up pocket notebook with a flourish and started recounting the events of the past two days.

'Now we are going to search the zoo,' said Sergeant Reg pompously, 'so you had better keep out of our way. We will be wanting to take statements from all of you in due course so don't leave the premises. I know a conspiracy when I see one.'

Now Walt is not a person who angers easily, but he had clearly had enough. He raised himself up to his full height and glared at the sergeant. 'Sergeant Reynolds, this is a private zoo full of dangerous animals. If you think for one moment that you and your constables are going to start rooting around in here on your own and without a warrant, you are very sadly mistaken. I would further advise you not to make any further accusations or insinuate in any way that any persons here are involved in your conspiracy theory. I would remind you that your Chief Inspector is one of our Trustees and if you persist, I can see you becoming the oldest constable in this district or tending your petunias on extended gardening leave. Do we understand each other?'

The cavalry had arrived. Good for you, Walt.

'Only doing my duty,' came the stock phrase in response.

'Ben, do you know anything about this, if so tell us now,' said Walt calmly.

'I ask the questions here.' Reg raises his ugly head again.

'Shut up,' Reg, yelled Walt, 'my staff, my place, my questions.'

'So, Ben.'

'As I told the sergeant, Mr Whitlam I have not seen the boy, not since he was taken away a few days ago.'

Mabel put her head around the door. 'Joe and Molly are here,' she announced.

'Send them in, Mabel, the more the merrier.'

'Oh, and Spencer has arrived as well.'

That's all we need, I thought. I had visions of balancing on the prow of a whaler with harpoon poised ready for a surfacing Spencer.

'What's going on?' said Spencer.

'Sergeant says he's escaped again and you are the chief suspect, Spencer. You could be in trouble,' I said mischievously.

'It wasn't me, whatever it was,' cried Spencer.

'Don't wind him up, Ben, I know you might think it's funny but the sergeant here may take it seriously,' said Walt, 'tell you what, I will allocate one keeper for you and each of your constables, and they will go with you to any enclosure so you can search the whole place. How about that. Mind the crocodile, he hasn't been fed for a week and he likes anything in dark-blue.

'That was a joke. Christ, Ben, It's rubbing off on me.'

'Well, Mr Whitlam, there is not anything more for me to do, so I will get on with my job. No doubt Spencer will look after the ladies or they are welcome to wait in the restaurant and have some refreshment,' I said.

'Good idea, carry on, Ben.'

While Spencer chaperoned the three ladies to the restaurant, I gathered Joe and Molly together and found a quiet place in the copse behind the baboon enclosure.

'Don't know about you two, but I am not going to lie to the police.'

'You already have,' said Joe.

'No, I said very carefully that I hadn't seen him which was true. I am hoping he keeps his head down and they don't think about searching the island.'

'Joe and I spent most of last night talking after you left. We may have come up with something. So, here is our idea. We know the lad is special, they don't. All they see is a wild boy who they cannot contain or control. Mabel told us before we went in that he had attacked a staff member and broken something. Not sure what we can say about that last bit.

What if we put to Ms Marjorie that we will foster the boy? We have three bedrooms, not that he will probably use it, he can come and go to the zoo by the back gate without anybody really noticing. We will be responsible for his welfare and behaviour. Joe and I are after all a couple in a committed relationship.'

'Does that mean I have to marry you, Molly?'

'Of course, Joe,' she winked at me.

'The ultimate sacrifice,' moaned Joe.

'Miserable sod,' replied Molly.

'We would put it to them that we are actually helping them with a difficult problem for which they do not have a solution or probably the staff to deal with it.

'If we can get past social services, we think the police will back off.

'So that is the general plan. What do you think?'

'Brilliant,' I said.

'One thing and this is going to be your job… You sort Spencer out.'

'You want me to kill him, break his legs, how about a one way trip to the tigers?'

'No, you just have to bring him into the loop. We have no idea how. Your baby. Good luck!'

I'm going to need it. An idea was already forming in my mind but it involved being nice to Spencer. I will have to run with that however distasteful but Spencer has an Achilles heel – Marjorie. Win her over, win him over.

The search for the boy took all day and much as I envisaged, no trace of him was found. Whether he slept through the whole thing or saw them coming and hid in the depths of the hut, I do not know but we had bought ourselves some valuable time.

Joe, Molly and I met up at our table when the SWAT Team had left.

'I think we need to keep him hidden for a couple of days before we say anything to the Authorities otherwise it's going to look a bit obvious. Even then, we have to get our timing right,' I said.

The next two days dragged, as we just wanted to get on with our plan. In the meantime, we could coax Larry off the island for meals when there was no one around. Then on the third night, we put our plan to him.

Molly held his hand gently smoothed his hair off his brow and said to him, 'Larry, you know we like you very much. We would like to care for you and we are going to ask these people who took you away whether they will let us look after you. We know you want to be in or near the animals and we live just behind the zoo. We have a spare bedroom which you can use if you wish, but you must pretend that you are sleeping there even if you are not. How does that sound to you?'

No words, but his smile said everything.

'Is that a deal? But Larry, we can't make any promises, but we will try our best.'

The following day was a range of meetings. First Joe and Molly put their plan to Walt. Apparently, so they told me after, Walt knew about their relationship. Joe told me that he had caught them "canoodling" in the restaurant store one night and their personal details on file with the same address had just confirmed it to him. Mabel knew. Then Mabel knew everything that went on.

I started the ball rolling with Spencer who regarded me with great suspicion and I suspect I was overdoing things a bit especially greeting him like a long lost brother.

'You want something,' he said, 'or you have done something, I have a nose for these things.'

You certainly have a nose, I thought, *you could drill holes in the garden with it or join a woodpecker colony.*

The magic words sprang from my lips. 'I can see how much Marjorie likes you, Spencer, and we can all see how much she likes you. It's a pity that she has this trouble with the boy on her plate, I wonder if we can help her out somehow.' *Machiavelli, eat your heart out,* I thought.

The suspicious look immediately vanished from his face. 'Yes,' he said thoughtfully, 'we should help her with this, she is hoping to be promoted and it would help a lot.'

BINGO!

'Problem is, Spencer, we don't know where he is,' I lied, 'but we are pretty sure that he is going to turn up some day. He just loves the animals.'

'I know you think I am a bit of an ass,' he said, 'and maybe I didn't do the right thing before, but I have watched him and he seems to have a very special way with the animals.'

A chrysalis turning into a butterfly, an ugly duck turning into a swan and Spencer, at last, joining the human race.

The "A" team met up again that evening at their table alongside Larry happily munching through a leathery burger, to compare notes.

'Now for the big one,' said Joe, 'do we tell them that he has turned up, then put the proposal to them or do we do it the other way around.'

'My vote is that we do the first option even if it scares Larry or it will look very fishy,' I said.

'Ben's right,' said Molly.

'So, it's agreed then, better tell Larry,' said Joe, 'you can tell him, Molly.'

'Larry,' she said, 'you remember that we told you we had a plan, well, it is time to put it into action. There is a danger that they may take you away again. If they do, you must not forget that we will be outside trying to get you out and you must have patience. If you do not, they may take you away somewhere we can't find you. Do you understand?'

The boy reached out and held hands with Joe and Molly. He smiled and nodded.

The next morning, we got Mabel, who was now in on all of this, to call social services. She told her that Larry had turned up the no worse for wear and he was at that very moment being given a hearty meal at the zoo. She also said that the presence of the police might scare him and cause him to run off again.

Well done, Mabel.

Mabel told us that Ms Hoare would be coming around immediately and she would be coming alone.

Mabel, you are a star.

Chapter 7
Swimming in Mud

'I will call you when she arrives,' said Mabel, 'but don't be too far away. Not a lady to be kept waiting. I will have the meeting room ready for you. Mr Whitlam is away on a conference.'

We were in fact waiting outside and could have shouted a reply through the door so we went in.

'Blimey, I didn't even call you.'

'We were outside, bit nervous.'

'You go on in to the meeting room, and I will bring in some tea or coffee when she arrives. Oh! Here she is already.'

We went into the meeting room which led off the reception office. There is nothing extraordinary about it. Table with eight chairs, sideboard with a telephone on it and a whiteboard on the wall one end in case someone wanted to visually explain something.

'Good morning, Ms Hoare, how are you?' I said.

She looked down her nose at me with a hint of wariness. 'Fine, thank you.'

'And how is the young lad?' said Molly.

'I will be perfectly honest with you but he is a most unusual case. Calm one minute until everybody thinks he is settling in, then he will make a bolt for it.' Frankly, the staff has never seen anything like it. He's cunning as well. Twice he has got out and each time, there has been some sort of ruse he has concocted. So he is clever. Will not speak, will not sleep in a bed, will not cooperate.'

'So,' said Joe, 'what actually happens in these cases?'

'Eventually, the child is taken off to a more secure unit. There is one about 100 miles from here.'

'A juvenile prison, you mean,' said Molly.

'I wouldn't call it that, it's really for their own protection.'

'About the assault and damage he caused. The police seem to take a very serious view on this,' I said.

'The police are there to back us up and sometimes and sometimes, we are glad they do.'

A sudden knock and a ferrety face appeared around the door. 'Can I come in,' said Spencer, 'I need to be in on this.'

'Of course, Spencer,' said Ms Hoare, 'if you think you can add anything.'

'Yes, Marjorie, I mean Ms Hoare, I am deputy head keeper and this affects the zoo.'

Obviously, this was just Spencer being nosy and an opportunity to show off in front of Marjorie, so I kept my mouth shut for once. Who knows, it might help.

'We were just trying to get to the bottom of the incidents at the children's home, Spencer and Ms Hoare was hopefully going to enlighten us.'

'Well, the two broken windows are neither here nor there, in fact one of them was caused by a member of staff who was trying to catch him, so I would not be too concerned about that.

'The assault happened when a male member of staff caught him and picked him up and was rewarded with a kick in the shins. Painful, but maybe a case of a bruised ego more than anything.' The head of our department is prepared to overlook it. She is due to retire next month, and I do not think she wants the aggravation.'

'Ms Hoare is hoping to head the department when her boss retires,' confided Spencer, 'she has already had the interview, she's really good at her job you know.'

Now that is a potentially useful snippet of information, I thought. One to be tucked away for the future. Might be useful.

'Thank you,' Spencer, 'for the vote of confidence but that has really nothing to do with why I'm here.

I understand that you have an idea. Does this involve all of you?'

'It really involves Molly and me,' said Joe. 'Ben is here because he was the first one who found him, and the boy has been helping him around the zoo.'

'I have to tell you in confidence that Molly and I are in a committed relationship and live together just over the hill behind the zoo. We have been together for over ten years.'

The look on Spencer's face was an absolute picture. His jaw dropped and his eyes popped. 'Nobody told me, why was I kept out of it, I bet everybody else knew.'

Paranoia had reared its ugly head, or in Spencer's case, a double ugly head.

'It had nothing to do with you or our work here, Spencer, even Ben only found out yesterday by accident.'

'So, you are in fact married,' said Ms Hoare.

'Not exactly,' replied Molly, glancing sideways at Joe, 'but I have expectations. It's a sort of civil or common-law marriage. The main thing is that we are a couple and committed and have a stable lifestyle and future.'

'OK,' said Ms Hoare, 'I get it, and what is the point of this?'

'The point is,' said Joe, 'that we are in a position to offer the lad a home.'

'You mean you want to adopt him, and if you do, I can tell you there are all sorts of problems. We have to find out who he is and where he comes from. You can't go adopting a child who belongs to someone else. Then there are questions on your suitability, ages being one. Then there have to be checks on the accommodation, schooling, dietary considerations—'

'Can I interrupt you there?' said Joe, 'What we had in mind was a kind of fostering arrangement. I can list the benefits.'

'First, the boy loves animals and we can keep him occupied here at the zoo out of harm's way. He will "shadow" Ben on a daily basis. Ben says he is very useful and an amazing talent with the animals. He will be covered by the zoo umbrella insurance policy.

'Second, we have a three-bedroom bungalow nearby and he would have his own room and be able to treat the place as his home.

'Third, we will feed and clothe him and make sure he is comfortable and happy.

'Fourth, he would be out of your hair until such time as you or we find out where he came from.'

'This is very irregular. You must remember that we have regulations, responsibilities and higher authorities to satisfy. I must admit that your idea has some merit, but there are a lot of steps to go through. I need to think about it, consult with my superiors and also talk to the police. In the meantime, the boy must stay in the children's home, and it would be most important that you impress upon him that there should be no more escapes or incidents or it will be completely taken out of my hands.'

'Understood,' said Joe, 'and thank you for hearing us out. Would it be possible for him to come here during the day? Ben will come and pick him up and have him back by whatever time you say.'

'I think that is a step too far at present, it is a question of divided responsibility, so no.'

'Can we come to visit him then?' I said.

'It is not encouraged in case it unsettles the other children,' she said, 'but I will confirm it with Ms Cartwright and let you know.'

'Ms Hoare really knows what she is talking about.'

'Yes, Spencer, I think we all gathered that and have very confidence in her experience and professionalism,' I said.

'Good,' said Ms Hoare, 'I will wait here while you fetch him. Shall we say thirty minutes? Then I will take him to the home with me.'

Joe and Molly left.

'Perhaps you would like a coffee or tea while we wait,' said Spencer.

'No need to hold you or your colleague up from your work.'

'No, it is my pleasure,' said Spencer, 'you are our guest here, but I'm sure Ben will want to get back to things.'

What a creep.

'No, I will wait here for the three of them to return.'

'So,' Ms Hoare, 'how long have you been working for social services, sounds like a difficult profession.'

I can creep with the best of them, I thought.

'About eight years now, ever since I left University.'

'What did you take there, may I ask?'

'I did an undergraduate degree with honours in sociology then a masters in clinical psychology.'

'Wow, you really are a force to be reckoned with, Ms Hoare, by the way, did you know that one of our trustees is the councillor responsible for social services. Yes, he's a regular visitor here, brings his family here often and he even sponsors one of our animals, the red panda.'

'I didn't know that,' said Spencer.

'And why should you, Spencer, the red panda is one of my charges, in fact, Councillor Burrows will be here this coming Sunday. The red panda is a very shy creature and last time he came, it was hidden from sight so he was getting worried so I said to him, don't worry Councillor, next time you come, I will personally take you into his cage.'

'Thank you, Ben,' he said to me, 'very kind of you. I like people who are helpful, committed to their jobs but have a flexible approach to problem solving.'

'I didn't know you knew the Councillor, Ben,' said Spencer.

'Ah, but you know so many other things, Spencer, you are our mine of information on anything animal. Walking encyclopaedia. Ms Hoare, you really should spend a day with Spencer and go around the zoo with him, that is, if you are interested. I'm sure he would be delighted. Wouldn't you?'

'Absolutely,' he gabbled, 'any time, Marjorie, I can't tell you how pleased I would be.'

'Thank you, Spencer, I will take you up on that.'

'Anyone wants more tea or coffee,' shouted Mabel through the half-open door.

'No, we're fine, thanks,' I said. 'Ms Hoare, may I call you Marjorie, so, you are up for promotion. It would be very silly of the department to recruit someone from outside given your experience and now you have got this issue to add to your portfolio. I must tell the Councillor on Sunday what a good job you are doing in such trying and unusual circumstances.'

I think I might just have heard a muffled guffaw from the reception office. Well, I was laying it on a bit thick.

'Thank you, Ben, yes do call me Marjorie, I like to think that I am on top of my job and could lead the department to greater efforts.'

Mabel shouted, 'They're back.'

I went outside. Larry was standing between Joe and Molly holding their hands while she was trying hard to hold back her tears.

'We have had a good chat with Larry and he has promised to be good,' said Joe.

I crouched down in front of him. 'While you are away, I am going to take good care of your animals and we will be doing all we can to get you back here with us.' He disengaged his hands and gave me a hug.

'Come on, young man,' said Marjorie, 'off we go.'

No wave goodbye, just a slight turn of his head. A strange child indeed.

'I will see you two in a bit for lunch. I just have to pop back into the office for some visitor forms.'

'Well, that was a performance for the Oscars,' laughed Mabel, 'I was watching her face through the door. Hook, line and sinker. Played that one really well. How much of that twaddle was actually true? None, I bet. Even Spencer likes you now. I can see you being best man at the wedding.'

'I wonder why we have never gone out together, Mabel, you have a disgusting mind like mine.'

'You couldn't afford me and besides my husband's huge.'

I went off down the hill to join the other two for lunch.

Good as her word, I got a message from Mabel that Marjorie had called and said it would be all right for us to visit

Larry but no more than two at a time and we should call Ms Cartwright first.

A week went by with daily visits from two out of the three of us at a time. We could see that Larry was struggling with his promise to behave, so we made sure he had detailed reports on the animals which seemed to calm him a lot.

Eight days after the last meeting with Marjorie, Mabel called to say that Marjorie had asked for a meeting at three that afternoon. She added that Walt had returned; he had been briefed and he would be sitting in.

The time dragged until three o'clock came around, and we were now sitting in the meeting room waiting to see what fate beheld us and the boy.

'I understand that Councillor Burrows is a friend of yours,' said Walt, peering ominously at me, 'I did not know that, apparently you are going to let him cuddle the red panda. Do I sense some skulduggery here, Ben, or am I just getting old and paranoid?'

'Here's Ms Hoare and Spencer,' announced Mabel, 'can they come in?' *Saved by the Mabel,* I thought. Well, not saved, but it will give me some time to try and think up something.

'Shall we have a chat about this later, Ben?'

'Yes,' Mr Whitlam.

'Come in and sit down, Ms Hoare, sorry to miss you the other day, but I was away. I have been brought up to date with what has been going on and I can tell you now, that their proposal is a good one and I hope you will concur.'

'Thank you, Mr Whitlam, I can tell you that the last few days have not been easy and there has certainly not been a consensus in the departments. Thankfully, the police have, as I thought, left the final decision to our department and there will be no repercussions as to the assault and damage issues.

'The deciding factor came from my superior whom I am glad to tell you is supporting my application to replace her and had in turn been given a report by councillor Burrows on this situation before I could brief her myself.'

Finishing the last bit, she looked sideways at me for just an instant with what I presume was the hint of a smile. Maybe my imagination, hard to tell but the glance was not lost on Walt whose eyebrows raised as he looked again at me.

'We cannot accept that this arrangement would meet with normal practise,' she began, 'but there exceptional circumstances here which merit, shall we say, a more flexible approach.'

Again glancing at me.

'In essence, the department are prepared to accept your proposal,' she continued, 'but there are some very strict conditions and we have prepared a contract which I will paraphrase for you. The conditions are not up for negotiation.

'Let me tell you first that the contract is for a temporary fostering arrangement until such time as the parents and/or home of the child are found. After one year, if the said parents and/or home have not been found then arrangements will be made for Joe and Molly to have first right of refusal to adopt him.

'Joe and Molly due to their ages must undergo medical examinations including blood tests plus a psychological evaluation which is standard practise. An inspection will be made by the department of the proposed residence which is also standard practise. Then if all being well, the contract can be entered into. There are a number of forms for you both to sign and have witnessed. Copies will be given to you for safekeeping. I cannot underestimate the importance of the paperwork involved or adherence to the procedures that go with them.

'Luckily,' she continued, 'I have anticipated your response and I have brought some of the forms with me.' She opened her briefcase and pulled out a rather thick wad of papers.

'Now,' she said, 'as you are not married, there are two sets of everything to complete.

'Form 283A requires your personal details which include information on your parents and immediate family, education, addresses where you have lived for the past 20 years etc.

'Form 63 requires confirmation from your bank about your financial stability and you to fill out details of savings, investments etc.

'Form 129 Edition 5 requires your full medical history including allergies.

'Form 129 Edition 11 gives us permission to check your medical records.

'Form 333 gives us permission to get your police report. You have to do this as well direct with the police so this is a double check we do.

'Form 1094 is permission for you to attend a psychiatric examination. We can't be too careful. The reverse side has some small visual tests which will be analysed by the psychiatrist at your meeting. They may look a little strange but I assure you they are the result of many years of research.

'Form 6 is basically a questionnaire which asks why you think you are suitable to foster a child. This needs two referees of good standing like a clergyman, judge, magistrate or policeman. Someone who has known you for at least five years.

'Finally, form 900 is to exempt the Department from any loss, damage or legal action resulting from the placement. This form has to be signed, dated and counter signed by a notary.'

'Gosh, never seen so much paperwork,' murmured Joe in horror, 'it's like swimming in mud.'

Ms Hoare ignored this and continued,

1. 'The child will be delivered to the care of Joe and Molly and he will abide at their residence. They will feed and clothe him and be responsible for his actions and behaviour at all times.
2. 'The child will retain the name Larry until such time as his real name is known and may take Joe's surname as his own should he need it.
3. 'He may work at the zoo who will be legally liable for him. His hours off working must however be limited to that prescribed by law for a minor.
4. 'The child will attend the local school during their regular hours unless the Education Board can be satisfied that he can receive an equivalent home-school based education.

5. 'The child has been medically examined and has deemed to be in good health. They have assessed his age at 12 years old or thereabouts. We have set his birthdate as today's date.
6. 'The department will review your progress on a weekly basis for the first three months and quarterly thereafter.

'No doubt as time progresses, you will have some questions or concerns and if so, you should contact me at the department. Your secretary here has my details.

'I will bid you good day and wish you the best of luck. It is a very strange situation and I think you may need it.'

Chapter 8
Life Changes

The following weeks were full of revelation, surprises and delights. Not so for Joe and Molly who spent their leisure hours grinding through the mass of form filling.

'I can't remember what I did last week,' complained Molly to me, 'and she wants us to go back 20 years or more.'

'Don't envy you that, Molly, I hate paperwork.'

'Now, if we were to get married,' she said looking at Joe, 'the form filling would not be so bad.'

'Call coming in,' said Joe, clutching his mobile phone to his ear, 'have to take this outside, may be important.' He rushed out of the restaurant.

'Moves fast for a big chap,' I mused, 'wonder who called?'

'No one, you dope,' said Molly, 'just a ruse, he's done it before. Silly thing is, he knows it's just a matter of time before it happens. Never been married before, unlike Joe, so it would be nice.'

'Think you are going to need some drugs for him.'

'Don't you think I haven't thought of that? Problem is if they are too strong, he won't be able to stand up or speak and too weak, I'll be chasing down the road after him.'

'Speak to James, he's good at balancing sedatives. How much does Joe weigh? I'll fetch the gun.'

'I've seen you with that gun,' replied Molly, 'remember the sun bear you shot in the bum. Except you missed and hit him in the right testicle. Poor creature and can hear his howls now.'

'Yes, OK, I was trying to forget that one. I can't walk past his cage without him going mad. I actually walk around the back to avoid him. Heaven knows what would happen if he ever gets loose.'

'Bet you thought I was trying to avoid you,' said Joe re-appearing, 'that was Ms Hoare. She has agreed to our further suggestion that the boy be allowed to come here every day as a special consideration as long as he is picked up by eight each morning and has to be back for six. I gather than Larry is "restless". Reading between the lines, I think she means he is getting unmanageable again.'

'I am so happy,' chirped Molly, 'I have had sleepless nights thinking about that poor boy in that place, when does this start?'

'Tomorrow,' said Joe.

Breakfast over we went our separate ways on our self-allotted tasks and strolling up the hill, I duly arrived at the visitor centre.

Now the visitor centre is a single-storey octagonal building in which parties of visitors, many school parties, learn about various animals. We are all called on to give a talk on the animals in our own care and this often involves bringing in some of the creatures to demonstrate.

Why the building is octagonal, I do not know, maybe so the kids can't hide in corners so easily. In the centre is a small stage or dais on which there is a perch as a permanent fixture and a tall, wooden table on which to place exhibits.

That day, there was a group of school kids, probably about twenty, not sure as they move around to count accurately, and on the dais, capuchin monkey in hand, or more accurately on the end of a leash, was a vision of pure loveliness clad in a grass-green jumpsuit. My mum always told me it was rude to stare. Forgot all about that. I just stood there entranced. It wasn't just the fact that she was very beautiful, I had seen plenty of beautiful girls, but this one had character that oozed out of every movement and expression. She had a very clear almost musical voice. I could not take my eyes off her. Did I realise at that moment I was hooked? Probably not.

She was clearly not their teacher as there were two of them standing in the background probably trying to plan their escape. Not one of our staff so she must be one of the many visiting specialists.

I was enthralled and a voice next to me suddenly whispered, 'Your mouth is open, Ben, and you are drooling.'

'Sorry,' I stuttered, 'didn't realise. Who is that great looking girl over there?'

'Which one?' replied Freddy. 'Only joking. That's Cecilia, biologist, brains coming out of her ears. Been here before. So, today she is giving the school kids talks on the primates. She has an MA in that subject so she knows what she is talking about.'

'How do you know her, Freddy?'

'Known her for years, Ben, real handful, bites your head off as soon as looks at you.'

'Sounds like you had a bad experience with her,' I said, 'she looks very nice.'

'Looks can be and in this case are deceiving, Ben, walk away while you can.'

'How long have you known her, Freddy?'

'Over twenty-eight years. Lived with her for eighteen of those.'

'She doesn't look that old.'

'She's twenty-eight.'

'I don't get it, Freddy.'

'Trust me you don't want it, Ben, she's my sister.'

'Oh God, sorry, Freddy, I didn't mean—'

'Forget it, Ben, I suppose you want me to introduce you. Already lost two close friends who thought they could take her on, so I would rather not lose you as well but I can see that look and you are not going to be deterred. Just remember, I warned you.'

We stood there together and I must have been staring as now and then, I got quick suspicious-looking glances from the girl. I was in fact in a semi-dreamlike state, kind of reminiscing and daydreaming at the same time.

My mind wandered back to the talks I had with my father when I was growing up. He never got to the "birds and the bees" either because he thought I already knew or more probably because he was too embarrassed.

'Dad wants to speak to you in the greenhouse,' said Mum, 'he's waiting.'

The greenhouse was halfway down our garden and was where my father would impart his knowledge to me from time to time. Never often, when it did come, it was concise and conclusive.

Why the greenhouse, I never found out, but it was his haven and he probably knew that once in there with the sliding door shut, my mother would not interfere with his speech and the pearls of wisdom contained therein.

'Mother says you are broken up about that girl you play tennis with,' he said, 'no point in moping about.'

'I like her very much, I can't understand what I did wrong, she just told me that it was over.'

I was fifteen and these things are extra important at that age being already self-conscious and insecure.

'Look here,' said Dad, 'I am going to give you one of the best pieces of advice you will ever hear. Women are different from us.'

'Yes, Dad, they have those nice bumps on the front of them,' I said flippantly.

'No, son, there are other things.'

'I haven't got to those bits yet, Dad, but I have ambition.'

Exasperated, he said, 'If you are going to be a smartass and not listen, then I'm wasting my breath.'

'Sorry, bit embarrassed.'

'Women are different. But they don't know they are different. They think differently, they react differently, they behave differently. Now you will find that they will try and change you. This is not because they are despotic or bossy, although some are. It is an inability to look at themselves rationally.

'Sometimes this is funny, although you certainly must not laugh at them. Other times, it is very annoying but you must not show it.

106

'The secret of a happy life is to just go along with it. Smile inwardly at their idiosyncrasies but say…nothing. Got it?'

'I think so, Dad,' I said, not really having a clue what he was talking about. *What's that got to do with being chucked by my girlfriend?* I thought. *Mind you, I'm off to badminton club tonight and there's a new member there that I would like to get to know.*

Oh! The callowness of youth!

'Ben, are you still with us?' said Freddy.

'Sorry, drifted off there for a minute.'

'Listen, she's just wrapping up so come with me.'

The kids and their reluctant teachers went out through the front double doors and the girl complete with monkey on her shoulder went out the back.

'Cecilia,' called Freddy, 'hang on, someone I want you to meet.'

'Hi, Brother, who is this then?' she asked, eyeing me up and down.

'This is Ben, he is one of the two deputy head keepers and you have one of his family on your shoulder.'

'No family resemblance,' she said, 'but much cuter.'

'Thanks,' I said.

'Not you, the capuchin.'

Freddy gave me a "told you so" look.

'Freddy tells me you are a biologist and know a lot about primates.' *Not a great start,* I thought, *she must think my IQ and shoe size are about the same.*

'Yes and yes,' she answered, 'what else did he tell you. Let me guess. You want to keep away from her, eats men for breakfast, made his life a living hell.'

'Well, to be honest, he didn't mention the last bit.'

'Only because he forgot,' she said.

'I have to say, I have never seen a lovely speaker or heard such an interesting talk,' I gushed. I really wish I hadn't said that.

'Strewth,' she said, raising her eyes skyward, 'the missing link found at last.'

'Well, I've got to go,' the blushes in full flow, 'nice to meet you, I have to go and see to the gibbons.'

'Is that guy in charge of you?' I heard her say, as I retreated.

'No, we are colleagues, but we are in the same department,' said Freddy.

'What department is that? Knobs Anonymous.'

I broke into a run. 'To sanctuary,' my inner voice cried.

I had several sanctuaries but my favourite was Gibbon Island and that is where I headed. The gibbons had settled down after the Larry's departure but at times could still be peering towards the restaurant and main path. Or was it my imagination.

A nice, dry, sunny afternoon, I will climb a tree. Sure enough, two of the adults joined me plus two youngsters and they sat down near me occasionally approaching and stroking my arm or leg. This really is communing with nature and I shut my eyes for a moment.

'How do I get over there?' called a voice. 'I know you are there, I can see your foot.'

'Keepers only here,' I shouted back, 'not allowed.'

'Yes, I am, Mr Whitlam said so, it's Cecilia.'

'If you want to come here, you will have to swim across, mind the piranhas.' Not nice, but I was feeling slighted and this was a, OK childish, way of getting my own back.

She disappeared and I thought that was the last of that but I was wrong as she had evidently, so Molly told me, gone into the restaurant with some questions and had learned that the lake was in fact shallow and relatively benign.

I opened my eyes and heard a splash and there was Cecilia with her trousers rolled up way above her knees stepping very delicately into the water. Nice legs though.

She reached the island and clambered onto the dock log. 'Not very gentlemanly,' she said, looking up to roughly where I was sitting.

'Who told you I was a gentleman?'

'Oh, like that is it, can I come up the tree?'

'Find your own tree,' I replied, 'this one is just for knobs.'

'Sulking, are we?'

'Don't know about you, but I am.'

She burst out laughing.

'I am sorry,' she said, 'I have this sort of defence mechanism to ward off intruders.'

'You shouldn't be so bloody lovely,' I said.

'I can't help it. Can I come up now?'

'OK, but do it slowly, I have four of them up here and they don't know you. We were just having a "gibbon plus one love in".

'Can I join in?' she said.

'Me or the gibbons?'

'Don't push it,' she warned.

'I can see why you like it up here. You can see the world, but the world can't see you. What are you hiding from? Don't answer that, it's none of my business.'

'No, I can answer that. This, to me is what our zoo is all about. Protection without cages and this epitomises that. Being here with this family in their habitat is magical. The only pity is that we cannot have all the animals roaming around as free as these are here.'

'But the others are all in cages.'

'For the main, yes, they are, but this is an unusual zoo which was never built or developed as a tourist attraction. The animals here are either bred or reared in captivity that cannot be returned to a wild they have no experience of, or are endangered species that we encourage to breed and then hopefully introduce to their natural habitat. Even though they are in cages or enclosures, we try to make sure they are as large as possible and have natural features that they would find where they come from.

'These gibbons for example retain their instincts but they are all bred here or have been rescued as orphans from hunters and now they are safe. What we need now is a series of "half-way houses" where the animals can be sent to near enough where they came from and mixed with feral animals who could teach them how to survive.

'Sadly, this is a pipe dream as the logistics are finance involved are prohibitive and even if we could get over those hurdles, then the number who would survive would be minimal.

'So we do what we can and although not ideal, we look after all of them here the best we can.'

I gestured to one of the blond youngsters and sure enough, she crept over towards me, sat in my lap and put her long arms around my neck.

'She really trusts you,' said Cecilia, 'that's amazing.'

'If she didn't, her mother, who by the way is sitting next to you, would have something to say about it.'

'See if her brother, the little dark one will come to you. He might, you see, we are in their territory, so they feel more secure.'

She made a clicking noise and wiggled her fingers and sure enough, the young gibbon came toward her very gingerly. I thought the mother was going to reach out to prevent the little one from approaching but she simply stretched out her arm and placed it on Cecilia's shoulder. The youngster climbed into her lap now without hesitation.

'Why are some pale and some dark?' she asked.

'We don't know, it's something genetic like blue or brown eyes. There can be two dark parents and then one of their two babies or both can be light coloured.'

'You actually love them, don't you?'

'I don't tell them enough,' I said.

'Can we do this again?' she asked.

'Why are you a different person in a tree than on the ground?' I said.

'I'm out of my natural habitat.'

We climbed down from the tree after disentangling ourselves from the babies and mother and the three others who had joined us and clearly wanted us to stay.

'Hang on, I'll get the boat.' I moored it around the other side of the island so no one would know I was here. 'Old trick I learned from a friend.'

'Who's the friend?'

'You'll meet him soon, I hope. He is coming back tomorrow.'

'Back from where?' she asked.

'Too many questions, get in the boat.'

'Yes. Oh master,' she replied.

A few short strokes and we were back on the mainland. 'Cup of coffee? This is Molly.'

'I have met Molly already, she has already given me the lowdown on you.'

'I bet she has, Molly, what have you been telling her?'

'What's to tell?' said Molly enigmatically. A raised eyebrow and her wink said something different.

'I have to go now,' said Cecilia flashing her green eyes at me. 'Thank you for the tour, I mean climb, Ben. See you again.'

Molly and I watched her walk away waving her hand once without looking back. Joe arrived and watched her go.

'Who on earth was that,' he exclaimed, 'wow, never seen her before, she's like something out of modelling catalogue. Wow!'

'Put your tongue back in your mouth, look at the pair of you, I don't know.'

'Well, who is she?'

'That's Ben's new girlfriend,' said Molly.

'I wish. She thinks I'm a moron,' I said.

'Men,' exclaimed Molly, 'you really don't have a clue, do you? Come on now, time to eat.' Larry's coming back tomorrow and I will have his breakfast ready. Who's picking him up?'

'Ben is,' said Joe, 'I have to see Walt first thing.'

The following morning, I got up early as I couldn't sleep and made my way to the zoo on my bike. Then to the office, grab the keys and off to pick up Larry.

The children's home was only about a ten-minute drive away and I got there 20 minutes early. The front door was locked as usual so I rang the doorbell and a lady quickly appeared.

'You from the zoo, you're early.'

'Bad habit, come to pick up the boy,' I said.

'Here, sign this, he's in a bit of a mood.'

'What's he done?' I asked with that leaden feeling in the stomach that heralds bad news.

'He won't talk, won't eat, won't sleep in his bed and then spends hours making strange noises through the open window. Cats come, birds come, dogs come, even a fox with her cubs. Must have some sort of whistle in his voice that attracts them. Very odd. Creepy, if you ask me.'

'Happy to take him off your hands, ah! Here is the man himself.'

Larry broke into a run as he saw me and rushed into my arms. He was trembling for why I didn't know. He had obviously been waiting near the door. Now he had a big smile all over his face.

'See you at 6pm.'

'Don't rush back,' she said.

'Have you had breakfast, Larry?' I asked, getting into the van.

He shook his head.

'Well, I know who and what will be waiting for you.'

I was right. Fifty yards from the restaurant, Larry broke into a charge straight into the arms of Molly and virtually disappeared into her very ample bosom. She was in tears and I have to admit to choking a couple back myself.

'I'm going to fatten you up,' she said, 'you are too skinny.'

Munching through an impressive fry-up, Larry's eyes were alternatively on Molly, the island and me. The gibbons knew something because they were lined up on the bank. One even looked as though it was about to jump in and swim for it.

Last mouthful and he was off. No waiting for the boat or even rolling his trousers up. He just went straight into the lake, shoes, socks and all. Lot of hooting and what looked like a rolling mass of different coloured arms and legs and then it disentangled itself and bodies headed for the trees amidst noisy whooping and joyous swinging.

'Well, Larry's home,' said Molly, just as Joe appeared fresh from his meeting with Walt.

'He's back, thank goodness, I see, well I can hear anyway that he is on the island with his fans.'

'Have you finished with Walt?' I asked.

'Something and nothing. Just some new procedure for checking time sheets. Usually happens every year when it is budgeting time.'

'How are you two getting on with the fostering thing?'

Joe winced. 'I never want to see another bloody form in my life. Waste of paper. No wonder the brain forests are depleting. Still we have done everything we have to. Got all the forms signed, checked, double-checked, countersigned, notarised and submitted. Some we had to amend twice. Then we have had the necessary medical and psychological tests. Nearly lost it in the last one. The woman started showing me pages and pages of blobs asking me what I made of them. She frowned a lot so not sure how I did.

'We have just got to wait for Ms Marjorie Hoare, whom, I now hear has been promoted to head of department.'

'So, how is the new girlfriend, Ben, tried her out yet?'

'Don't be so crude, Joe, he'll want to take it carefully, do things properly—'

'Then try her out,' interrupted Joe.

'I know you want to get me fixed up but for your information, she is not my type. She is very lovely, intelligent and loves animals but she has a tongue like a scouring brush,' I said, 'too much trouble.'

'Not the Dunkirk spirit,' said Joe, 'thought you liked a challenge.'

'What's with the Dunkirk spirit, you think I'm going to get a little boat and drag her off some Normandy beach?'

Molly and Joe regarded at each other, slowly shaking their heads, with a look that told me that they did not believe me for one minute.

'Molly knows best,' said Joe, 'she sees things that others don't.'

'What's that meant to mean?' I asked.

'She is from the Moor, Ben.'

'So are the sheep and moorland ponies. I have even come across an adder or two,' I scoffed.

'You'll see, Ben, you'll see.'

'OK, Larry,' I called, 'that's enough, work time, you can come with me on my rounds. Leave your socks and shoes on the bank to dry. You'll have to keep your wet trousers on.'

That morning, I had a new spring in my step. Larry followed me everywhere being his usual very helpful self, the only problem was me having to keep back tracking to find him hanging over a fence to get nearer to the animals or just dawdling deep in thought. Behind him came a male peacock and two hens. The peacocks roam free in the zoo and the males give wonderful displays at certain times of the year. Behind then came two white Muscovy ducks and a Canada goose with a crippled leg. Oh, yes, and shadowing us in the bushes I espied a lemur who obviously was on a field trip from his island.

'Larry, will you try and catch that lemur and take him back where he belongs. Do it quickly before the rest of them decide to follow. I'll fetch a net.'

Larry shook his head then turned around, knelt on the ground, spread his arms out in a sort of open embrace and made a soft fluting whistling sound. The lemur bounded out of the nearby bushes straight to him and clung on. Larry trotted off with him to the lemur island bridge.

'I saw that,' said a voice. It was Cecilia.

'You here again,' I said, not looking at her.

'Yes,' she said, 'I'm here for a month, aren't you pleased?'

'Not particularly.'

'I thought you liked me.'

'What gave you that idea,' I answered.

'You let me share your tree.'

'Belongs to the gibbons, I just happened to be up there.'

'Still sulking?'

'No.'

'Sounds like it. Who's the boy, your son? Where's he going with that lemur? Why are all these birds following us?'

114

'Questions, questions. That's Larry. He is a trainee and he is not my son. I don't have one. I do not know why the birds are following us. Ask them.'

'Bit shirty this morning, aren't we? I have to go and prepare for the next lecture. There's a busload arriving at eleven and I have to mesmerise them with my speech. By the way, and that is why I came to find you. Mr Whitlam says you are in charge of the primates, so can I borrow a monkey please. A spider monkey to be exact, as I want to talk to the kids about their prehensile abilities.'

'They are a bit of a boisterous lot but there is one which you can borrow, as long as you promise to bring him back. He is a bit of a loner and has a disfigured face. Take Larry with you, he will be back in a minute once he has delivered the lemur.'

The minute turned into five then ten before he reappeared. 'By the look of you, you have had some sort of lemur-fest, Larry. I won't ask. Right, this is Miss Cecilia, she is a biologist and in about half an hour, she has to give a talk in the visitor pavilion. Your job is to go and fetch Raymond, then take him with you. Now, Raymond is quite placid but don't let the children grab hold of him in case they scare him.'

OK, got that, I will be along in a bit to see how you are doing. Remember Larry, you are in charge of Raymond.'

Off they trotted to the primate section where Larry and Cecilia would have to separate Raymond from the rest of the spider monkeys. Not a madly difficult task as Raymond would be on his own as usual but the hard part would be to stop the others trying to follow them out of the cage. *Still, I thought, Cecilia was an acknowledged primate expert and Larry had a way with animals.* Hang on, though. Cecilia might have the qualifications but I wonder whether she had ever had to undertake these sort of tasks before. In at the deep end!

I wandered off to see James as one of the giraffes had ripped a shin on the wire fence and found him and Freddy there waiting for me.

'This is going to take the three of us,' said James, 'did you bring that lad with you, he seems to have a calming effect on giraffes.'

'Not just giraffes, no, I didn't, he has gone off to fetch an exhibit with Cecilia.'

'We'll have to cope. Now, it is the female that is hurt and she will not leave the calf. If she gets excited and thinks her calf is in danger, she is likely to start trying to trample us. The plan is we separate them but they are on each side of the lattice fence so they stay in contact. Ben, you please feed the female from the gallery. I will be feeding the calf so our jobs are to keep them distracted. I have not fed either of them this morning so they should be hungry.

'Freddy, you go under the viewing gallery as it is too low and she will not be able to get to you under there. If she starts getting aggressive, you just retreat back under the gallery until we calm her down.'

'Not sure I like this plan,' said Freddy, 'looks like the only one in danger is me. Why don't I get the gun, give her a shot and take our time safely?'

'Because, one, it will traumatise the calf and two, sedating giraffes is not something I recommend unless absolutely necessary. You have to make sure they go down in a sort of recovery position and then you have to help them up afterwards. Probably more dangerous to all concerned.'

'Stop looking like that Freddy, if you wanted a nice safe job you should have stuck to handling poodles and budgies, stop complaining and just get on with it,' I said.

The wound needs to be cleaned and disinfected, then gauze applied then the elastic bandage you see over there that we use on horses legs.

'Take you two minutes, tops,' said James.

Twenty minutes later and a lot of scuffling, three false starts, Freddy dropping the gauze, Freddy not having had the foresight to find the end of the elastic bandage before he started, the job was done and Freddy emerged from under the gallery dripping in sweat.

'Hot work?' Freddy, asked James, 'Looks like we should hang you out to dry.'

'Didn't like the look in her eye.'

'Well, I have to be off. I want to see how Larry and Cecilia are getting on with the visitors. Left them in charge. Fingers crossed.'

As I walked away, Freddy caught me up. 'How are you getting on with my sister?' he said, 'She told me you and she were up a tree together. Full marks for originality. I never thought of that one.'

'Listen, she's absolutely stunning and I'm very surprised you are even related Freddy, your mum must be pleased at least one of you came out right. However, I am definitely not interested. Too much baggage with that one, have to spend a lifetime breaking down the wall she has built around herself.'

'Oh, so, you have given it a lot of thought then.'

'You just sort yourself out with Emily, Freddy, not sure whether you should give her one of your injections to quieten her down a bit. On a still night in the valley, she sometimes lends her voice to the night air when you two are at it. Luckily for you, only Joe and I have worked out that it is not the Howler monkeys.'

'Oh, God, I didn't realise, that puts me right off, I can tell you.'

'Will you tell Emily, or shall I?' I said, just to ram the point home. ''Scuse the pun!'

'No, no, I'll sort something out.'

'A gag maybe?'

Kick 'em when they're down.

Freddy turned right up the hill, ashen-faced no doubt on the way to his sweetheart. I didn't envy him the task ahead. I continued to the pavilion where Cecilia was in full flow. Raymond was sitting on Larry's head with his long arms cupped under his chin and his tail wrapped around his neck. *Great photo-op,* I thought. They were just finishing up and it looked as though my trust had been well placed. There was no blood on the floor, no fingers missing and no hysterical screams or recriminations. A good time had been had by all.

'We're going off to lunch now,' I said to Cecilia, 'but first, back in the cage with Raymond, unless you want to bring him with you, Larry.'

Larry nodded enthusiastically and we set off on the short trip to the restaurant. 'Can I come too,' said Cecilia.

'Free country, Cecilia, I'll throw you a bun,' I said.

'You are not coming into my restaurant with that, young man,' shouted Molly through the window, you stay outside and eat if you want.'

Raymond was attracting a lot of attention from visitors having lunch and the new arrival of the school kids from the pavilion added to the melee.

'He's very shy,' said Cecilia, 'hasn't said a word to me.'

'Us neither,' I said.

'Does he have something wrong with him?' she whispered.

'Not that I am aware of, we know what he wants?'

'Where does he come from?'

'At the moment, he lives in a children's home and we fetch him to and fro the zoo.'

'Doesn't he go to school?'

'He will do, things are getting sorted out for him, here's Molly and Joe looking like they found the cream.'

'Got some news,' said Joe, 'hello Cecilia, nice to see you three together getting along.'

'Humph!' I expelled.

'Miss Hoare, in her new position as head of department, has been having a meeting this morning with Ms Cartwright and they have agreed that until such time as the full formal agreement is ratified that young Larry, here, can stay with us under our protection and does not have to return to the home. Ms Hoare asks us to point out that this is a very unusual diversion. She used the word "flexible" several times and your name, Ben, came into the conversation.'

'Wow, hear that, Larry. So let's get this right. After work, you will go home with Joe and Molly. What you do after that is up to you and them. During the day, you will be my responsibility. How do you like that?'

A massive smile and Larry sprang out of his seat and launched himself on Molly still with Raymond clinging precariously to his head. Then, in turn, we all got the treatment including Cecilia.

'One thing,' said Molly, 'that does not come too.'

'You mean Raymond,' said Cecilia.

'Don't care what it's called,' murmured Molly, 'not in my house.'

Chapter 9
Resolution and Weirdness

The next few weeks, things had settled down to something approaching normality, if there ever was such a thing. Cecilia had been offered a full time position as Education Manager. We had never had one before as visitor education had been carried out on an ad hoc basis. Besides, I think Walt had developed a bit of a thing about Cecilia, then who wouldn't. We had been spending a lot of time together, but I had been sparring with her for almost four weeks now. To be honest, I couldn't get her out of my mind. Sad!

She caught me spying on her one day. I really don't know how. It must be some sort of sixth sense.

'I know you're there, Ben.'

'Oh! Hi, Cecilia,' I replied, feigning surprise.

'You were peering at me through that bush and you thought I didn't notice. Quite pervy.'

'Nothing like that, I was looking for something.'

'Yes, me, Ben, can I ask you something really personal?'

'What?'

'Do you like me? Are you attracted to me?' she asked.

'No, and yes,' I replied.

'I know you are attracted to me because you keep looking at me all the time, following me around or going to look for me. So, why don't you like me?'

'To be quite honest, Cecilia, you scare me. You have built a harsh shell around yourself and it is hard to get through. You are prickly and sarcastic and abrupt. So, I have built one around myself to protect myself. So our shells are bumping along against each other.'

'Oh! I see,' she said, 'not good. I don't realise I'm doing it sometimes. You may be right.'

She was silent for a minute.

'Ben, can I tell you a secret?'

'OK, what is it?'

'You have broken my shell and I now need help.'

'Go and see your brother, he's got some surgical glue and tape. He'll mend it in no time.' *I can be a cruel bastard sometimes,* I thought as I saw her misting up.

I walked off feeling really bad about how I had behaved. Sometimes when you want something so much and it is there for you, you just can't believe it.

I went off to rescue Larry from two of the rabble, or them from him. Not sure which.

'Where's Larry,' I said, 'I left you in charge of him.'

'Ben, come quick,' called a voice which I did not recognise at first, 'there's been an accident and it's bad. Daniel says to fetch you.'

I rushed up to him and we ran together down the hill in the direction of the big cats' enclosures. 'What's happened?'

'Don't know, Daniel just told me to get you quick.'

As I approached the tiger's enclosure, there was Daniel peering through the glass along with another one of the rabble.

'Thank God you came, it's Larry,' he said on the brink of hysteria, 'he got in with the tigers and they've killed him. Look you can see a leg sticking out under Kahn, the big male. Shall I fetch the Freddy and tell him to bring the gun?'

So this was the end, I thought, *all the time we believed he had some special relationship and it comes down to this.* My heart was in my stomach.

'Ben, look,' said Daniel, 'are my eyes playing tricks or did that foot just move?'

'I think you are right, if he is still alive, he is going to be badly hurt and the tiger is not going to give him up easily.'

Suddenly, a hand and arm appeared over the tiger's back followed by head and shoulders belonging to Larry. He rubbed his eyes.

'You come out of there, Larry, this instant,' I shouted.

While we were waiting, I said to Daniel, 'You know what he's been doing, don't you? He obviously went for a doze with the tigers and one decided he looked comfy and fell asleep on top of him.'

'Well,' said Daniel clearly relieved, 'I have seen everything now.'

'Now, young man, you have given us all a big scare, whatever made you go in there with them?'

He turned back toward the glass just as the big male strolled down the enclosure towards us. The tiger sat on his haunches and put his paw on the glass. Larry mirrored this with his hand. A loud purring erupted from the big cat. Larry giggled with delight.

'I just do not know what to make of this,' said Daniel.

'Ditto,' I replied.

It was lunchtime so Larry and I headed for the restaurant to meet up with Joe and Molly. Recently, Cecilia had made a point of joining us at mealtimes, much to the delight of Molly, but today was unusually absent.

I was telling Joe and Molly about what Larry had been up to when Freddy came in.

'Hi, everyone. Ben, can I have a word?'

I went outside with him, I saw Joe opening the sliding window slightly no doubt to earwig.

'It's Cecilia,' he said, 'what have you said to her. She is in the store behind my surgery bawling her eyes out. Never seen her like that before. Always been a hardass. Can't stand women crying.'

'I think it's my fault, Freddy, we had words earlier and I think I... What's the phrase? Spurned her advances.'

'Well, this is a first, I have seen her have men in tears, me included, I can tell you but I never thought I would see this. Can I ask you, Ben, are you serious about her? Inside I think there is something really nice. You just have to dig a lot.'

'The problem is quite simple, Freddy. I am head over heels with your sister, but I do not want to get hurt and she is so prickly.'

'Well, she's not now, so what are you going to do about it?'

'I really don't know, Freddy.'

'Go find her, you ass, bet she's still in the store.'

'Go get her, tiger,' shouted both Joe and Molly.

'Shut up, you two, you shouldn't have been listening.'

I made my way slowly up the hill back towards the surgery and went in. No one there, I tried the store. Pile of wet tissues but no Cecilia.

'Have you seen Cecilia?' asked James while we were passing.

'She looked a bit upset about something. She was heading for the restaurant area.'

I got back to the restaurant very quickly and to my surprise, no Cecilia but Joe, Molly, Larry and Freddy were standing outside.

In unison, they pointed to Gibbon Island. The boat was docked on the other side.

'Better swim for it, my luvver,' said Molly.

I did, rather, I waded.

'Are you there,' I called. Stupid question.

'Go away.'

'I want to talk to you…nicely. Where are you?'

'I'm up here, in the big tree.'

'Hang on, I'm coming up.'

I climbed up the tree. An easy climb about twenty feet and there she was.

'Cecilia, I am very sorry. Hurting you is the last thing in the world that I would want. Forgive me.'

She said nothing.

'Look, Cecilia, I would grovel, but twenty feet up a tree is a bit difficult so just imagine it please.'

That brought a small laugh. Phew!

I am going to come straight out with it Cecilia and take a risk. When I said I was scared of you, what I really meant, I was scared of you never liking me as much as I like you.

'So, you like me now,' she said quietly.

'I have always liked you from the first minute I clapped eyes on you.'

'I didn't feel like that about you at first,' she replied, 'you kind of grew on me.'

'So, are we OK, Cecilia?

'Yes, we are, Ben.'

'Will you come down now?'

'Only if you kiss me.'

Funny place for a first kiss!

'What are you two up to over there,' shouted Joe, 'the gibbons are getting restless and there's work to be done. Only kidding, you two stay there, I'll cover for you. Look out, you are about to get a visitor.'

Larry appeared at the bottom of the tree and was quickly jumped on by three gibbons. He climbed up to us with them hanging around his neck.

He got to our branch, disengaged one of them and passed her over to us. He then took hold of the gibbon's hand and then mine, gesturing for Cecilia to complete the circle.

I am not sure what happened at that moment though, as time has passed I have learned to understand it more. It was like a warm glow spreading up my arm and a tingling. We looked at each other, then to the gibbon and we knew. Nothing needed to be said.

Ten minutes later, we got down from the tree amid cheers from the other bank.

''Bout time you two sorted things out,' said Molly, 'thought I would never see the day.'

'Bloody matchmakers, we never stood a chance,' I said. Cecilia laughed.

I think we were too excited for lunch so I simply sat watching her. Red, auburn hair to her shoulders, green eyes and a figure to die for. *Wow, lucky, lucky me.*

'Back to work for us all,' said Joe.

Quick kiss with Cecilia and off we went our different ways.

'Can I borrow Larry again?' she asked. 'Got a presentation to do. Snakes this time.'

'If it's the cobra, make sure you get the right one. Larry knows which is which. Mind you, even the snakes like him, but we can't have them biting the visitors. You OK with that, Larry?' Larry nodded and waved a goodbye taking Cecilia's hand as they went.

As part of monthly chores, I had to check and agree time sheets which then went to Accounts. If the truth were told, I never really gave them a second look but just signed them off. I was doing that now when Spencer entered the meeting room.

'Hello, stranger,' I said with unusual bonhomie.

Spencer looked at me suspiciously. 'You're in a good mood. Well, that's good, as I have been waiting to have a word with you in private for a while now but picking the right moment has been tricky.'

'I am all ears, Spencer, what can I do for you?'

'Ben,' he said, 'knows you have never liked me and call me names, but can I be your friend?'

Gasp! 'What did you have in mind, Spencer?'

'Look, I know we haven't been close or seen eye to eye, but I do respect you and I have been a bit jealous of you in the past. Your popularity I mean.'

Flipping heck, where is this going, I thought, eyeing the distance to the door better let him ramble on a bit.

You have met Marjorie, well of course you have, Ms Hoare. Well, she is wonderful and we were getting on so well and then she got promoted and now seems to have cooled off. So, I need some help and advice.'

'If I may be so bold, Spencer, how far did you get with her?' I was not sure whether I wanted to hear the answer as visions of them entwined started to formulate in my head.

'We went to Exeter one day,' he replied.

'And?'

'We had a picnic in the cathedral close. It was very nice. I made sandwiches.'

'Not what I had in mind, Spencer, so do you have any ideas?'

I thought if I kind of modernised myself. What do you call it? Yes, a makeover.

There's a joke here somewhere but not the time and the place, I thought to myself, *as Spencer is looking particularly earnest.* There are hard tasks, even tougher tasks and impossible tasks but I have always been up for a challenge.

'Are you sure about this, Spencer, she seems the sort of girl who would be more attracted to the inner man,' I said.

'I thought so too, Ben, but frankly, I'm a bit desperate.'

'I am going to talk to Molly and Cecilia, if you don't mind. They will know about these things.'

'Thanks, Ben, you are a pal. I've never had a real friend before.'

'Steady on there, Spencer, you're beginning to creep me out.'

'Well, here's one for the record books. Two people pouring their hearts out to me in one day,' I said to myself.

That evening, I brief the ladies on the problem and ask their advice.

'From a female perspective, what's wrong with Spencer?' I asked.

'It's not like me to speak ill of anyone but I am at a bit of a loss on this one,' said Molly.

'How about you, Cecilia?'

Tricky one, but I would suggest something simple. The problem is not a makeover as such but to raise his confidence. He had the answer himself, just needs a push. Basically, he needs to be the old Spencer with new bits.'

'Like what?'

'New haircut and get him to use some product like conditioner. His hair now looks like he has just swam through an oil slick. Plus, new glasses. The ones he wears make him look like a geeky version of one of the Kray twins.'

'Who are the Kray twins, don't know them,' said Molly.

'They were east End London gangsters,' explained Cecilia, 'very nasty, one of them wore those horrible horn rim glasses. Spencer has the same ones.'

'Cecilia, will you go and have a word with him, I don't think I could keep my face straight.'

'I'll go and find him right now,' said Cecilia, 'no time like the present.'

Next day, I met up with Cecilia for breakfast. 'How did it go with Spencer?'

'Well, he certainly listened and seemed to take it on board and then went off at a tangent about going to the gym and tanning studio then buying new clothes,' she said.

'In all the years I have known him, I've never seen him in anything but his zoo stuff even when we have met up in the pub to celebrate something.'

'Don't worry, Ben, I think I talked him out of going too far and to just stick to those two items, hair and glasses.'

'OK, we'll wait and see.'

'Ben, can I ask you about Larry, I am so curious. You and the other two seem to protect him somehow, I mean, not physically, but when anyone asks, you deflect. Will you tell me?' she asked quietly.

'I think I have told you everything I know,' I replied.

'No, there is something more, can you not feel it, have you not noticed some little changes? When we walk past the animals with him, they seem to want to gather around. Even when he is not with me, I get the feeling that things are different. I am rambling because I can't explain it better.

'I have been thinking about this a lot. You remember when we were up the tree with Larry, did you feel a sort of pulse and warmth through your arms?'

'Yes, I thought it was a touch of cramp.'

'No, you didn't, you're deflecting again. He has a sort of power or influence over or with the animals and I really believe that at that moment, he passed some of it to us. Now, we may not be able to talk to the animals like he does…no, don't interrupt, you know this is true, but we have a kind of greater empathy with them. Does that make sense?'

'I suppose I have known this for some time, and now you put it into words I think you are right. One other thing I have noticed is, that when I go near the animals or even into their cages or enclosures, I have a new confidence that they will accept me. They lose their suspicion and nervousness. I can't explain it any better. He's someone very special.'

'I absolutely adore him,' exclaimed Cecilia, 'I love being with him and the animals. It's like I have a warm glow inside me. Maybe another part of that is you.'

Kissy time again. Damn! I'm getting addicted to this.

'See you later, lover boy,' called Cecilia, striding off away down the hill, 'see you later, I have to do a presentation again.'

I had got to the point now of trying to wean myself off chaperoning Larry everywhere and frankly, I was not sure at that moment exactly where he was and what he was doing. At first, I would write down in my little notebook who I had allocated him to and what tasks he should be undertaking. It had got to the point now where I loaned him out onto one of the keepers who after a given task would often "sub-let" him to another one or even, if the task was simple, to one of the Rabble. Without fail, he would find his way back to join us at meal times and I could then start the division of labour process all over again.

This particular evening, he had not appeared but I had heard from the keeper that, after cleaning out the elephants (a lengthy task), he wanted Larry to wash them down and file their nails. Apart from telling the keeper to get some waterproofs out for him, I left them to get on with it.

So that evening, I found myself alone with Joe and Molly at our table.

'You have something on your mind, my luvver,' said Molly. I let them both in on the discussion I had had with Cecilia earlier.

'So you have both felt it, I wondered when you would finally work it out,' said Molly smiling, 'it is nothing to be frightened of. Yes, it is strange, but then, so are many things. I have known from the first time I saw the lad that he is special. There are just some things that cannot be rationalised. They are what they are. Just accept it.'

'Molly,' said Joe, 'everyone are not like us and especially not like you, we must try and help them to understand.'

'What are you trying to tell me, Molly?' I said.

'He's a feyrling,' she whispered.

Chapter 10
The Legend of the Feyr

'He's a what?'

'A feyrling,' she answered

'No, Molly,' said Joe quietly, 'leave this alone.'

'No, he needs to know, Joe, Larry is very, very special, but he has already guessed some of it. We owe him the rest. Let me tell you what I know.'

'You know I was born on the moor, Ben, it is an odd place with a very strange history full of tales and legends. But to start, I must tell you that I come from a line who have what you may call "second sight". It is not something learned but something passed down from one generation from the next. There is nothing magical about it, but we can see and feel things that others cannot.

'I am told that we all have certain powers in us but in many, they lie dormant or are never developed. In some cases, they are even suppressed because that person is frightened of them.

'You know about dowsing. You have seen it here in the zoo when we want to find a watercourse or underground pipe-work. This is just one way it manifests itself, but you should know that there are those that can take this gift to a higher level. I have seen a lady who can tell you on a map, without even going to a particular location, the direction of flow, depth and even rate of flow. I have even heard of others who are developed even more and are much sought after by industri-alists to predict and find mineral and fuel sources. I am also told that two out of three people have the ability to dowse in various degrees. You should try yourself.

'Then there is the strange phenomenon of déjà vu. Many of us experience it, probably you have as well. No one can explain. Photographic memory, speed-reading and then we can then go on to other psychic "abilities" such as telekinesis, remote viewing and even teleportation.

'Many scoff at these things but I can assure you that they are very real.

'Larry has special gift and you have seen and felt this for yourself and it is quite simple – he can talk to animals.

'There are some on the fringe of our little "family" who have more than an idea that something strange has been happening. Cecilia has also seen and felt it. Even Spencer.

'Be warned, though, Ben, there is danger here, not just for Larry but for others like him and they will be hunted out, put on display, exploited and finally shunned and hunted just because they are different. We must protect the secret as far as we can.'

'Lot to take in, Molly, but I understand what you are saying. Maybe I have been denying this to myself but it is far too real and obvious to ignore,' I said. 'I do have a problem as Cecilia has not only been asking some very direct questions which I have been trying to duck, but she has already come to some of her own conclusions.'

'Cecilia is a special case,' said Molly, 'she has a gift of her own but she does not know it. She can be trusted but best not to tell her too much for now. I will leave that up to you. How are you two getting on? Seem happy enough.'

Our relationship has transcended from defensive sarcasm and goading into good-natured teasing. Happy is not the word for it.

'Enough about me. How did all this come about? Why the moor? What legends, what history?'

'Joe,' said Molly, 'I think it is time for Ben to meet a friend of ours who can explain things much better than you or I, this calls for a visit, I will call him. He will see us for sure. He is a great uncle of mine.'

'Who is this guy?' I asked.

'You will see, Ben, you will see. It will become much clearer. You will have to be patient.'

'I will go and call him now,' said Joe.

'There is another thing that you may have become aware of in yourself,' confided Molly.

'What's that, Molly?'

'Ben, over the last few weeks, have you not felt any different in yourself?' she asked.

'To be honest, the last few weeks have been a real roller coaster for me. Finding Larry, losing Larry, him turning up again, meeting Cecilia. She is enough by herself let alone everything else that's been happening,' I said.

'You have really fallen for her, haven't you? I'm so glad. Joe and I are so pleased that you have found someone at last.'

'I didn't think that Joe liked her that much, he's always telling me to be careful.'

'Ben,' she scolded, 'sometimes you can be incredibly thick. Why do you think he says these things? He cares for you. You are the son he never had. He is trying to protect you especially as he has seen the way you have behaved with some of your girlfriends in the past. He doesn't want to see you hurt.'

'What are you two plotting now,' said Joe, returning from outside, 'we can go and see him Sunday. We will have to find someone to look after Larry or we could take him with us. What do you think, Molly?'

'I just have a feeling that we shouldn't take him onto the moor. Can't explain it, but I think it's best.'

'I have got used to your feelings, Molly, they're usually right, so who's going to look after him.'

'I'll ask Cecilia,' I said, 'the two of them get on really well and I trust her.'

'Good choice, Ben, but be careful you do not tell her too much or she will want to come as well. By the way, don't tell her what we have been speaking about here, until you have been given the wider picture.'

'Who are we meeting?' I asked.

'You'll see, you'll like him,' said Joe.

'Where are we going?'

'We are going to a small village, well a hamlet really on the edge of the moor. He has lived there since he retired.'

'I will go and find Cecilia,' I said, 'see you later.'

'You told him too much, Molly,' said Joe, after I left.

'I haven't told him enough, Joe, you are going to have to be very careful with him when he finds out what we have only been hinting at. You are going to have to be very gentle with him. I think we both know Ben well enough to know how he will react.'

I wandered from the restaurant, up the hill in the direction where I had last seen Cecilia and Larry heading. First guess: the primate house, second guess: the primate house. I can't tell you I was hurrying. Too much on my mind. Was this all true or some fantasy that I was becoming party to? Some of it rings true. I had witnessed the old farmer who the maintenance guys call on to look for underground burst pipes; I had even seen them in their fields walking up and down with twigs or metal rods or even weighted, acnes so I had no problem with that one.

Then there was that television programme I had seen about that Israeli guy, Geller, who had been quite a personality bending spoons and mending watches but had apparently made a fortune from remote dowsing for big mining companies. I could go with photographic memory and speed-reading. I was actually naturally fast myself but I was having a lot of trouble digesting the rest of it.

Sooner, than I expected, I reached the primate house. This was one of the older buildings in the zoo. It had a symmetrical plan with an entrance and exit doors. These were handy as the monkeys are a "must-see" attraction so at peak times, we would station one of the rabble to filter people through. Every animal compound has an outside enclosure and an inside house. The inside house is to give the animals some privacy and also to lock them in when we are cleaning the outside enclosure and vice versa.

Sure enough, Larry was walking around inside the spider monkey enclosure with Raymond on his head deep in conversation with the other monkeys in his strange whistling and fluting voice. I had got quite used to it now and it was almost looking normal to me. However, we were careful in front of others particularly visitors.

'Where's Cecilia, Larry?' I called.

Without looking around, he gestured over his shoulder then carried on with what he was doing. 'Are you telling them all off, Larry?' He turned his head and nodded. *Looks like the others are picking on Raymond again,* I thought, *and Larry is reading them the Riot Act in "spiderese".*

'There you are, Ben, do you see what he's doing? I have been watching him from inside. Amazing. He has a gift. There's something I need to talk to you about…him,' she exclaimed.

Little do you know, I thought. 'Got a favour to ask you.'

'Will you look after Larry on Sunday, please?'

'What about Joe and Molly, don't they look after him weekends?'

'The three of us have to go somewhere.'

'Can I come too?'

'No, you have to look after Larry.'

'What if I say no?'

'It's important.'

'It's about Larry, isn't it? My nose is twitching,' she said.

'And a very fetching nose it is too,' trying a pathetic attempt at deflection.

'Now I know you are up to something, is it a big secret?'

'Look Cecilia, much as I love you, I can't tell you now, but I promise we will fill you in when we get back.'

'What did you say, did I hear right?'

'Yes, I said we would fill you in when we get back.'

'Not that bit.'

'What bit?'

'You said you loved me.'

'Damn, must have slipped out. Probably thinking about someone else.'

'You honestly think you are going to get away with that,' she laughed.

'Ruined at last,' I sighed.

'Am I really that bad?'

'Yes.'

'Do you want a thick ear?'

'I can think of something better,' grabbing her.

Kissing Cecilia was less like a hobby and more like a career, and we were quite carried away when I felt a tug on my trousers and looked down. Larry was looking up at us with a cheeky smile on his face then did a kissy moue at us. We both pulled him to us. Larry likes hugs.

Then he put his hand up, picked up Raymond, put his arms around him and gave him a big smacker on the lips.

'Looks like we have ruined Larry as well,' I said.

'You think that's bad,' replied Cecilia, 'by the look on his face, I think Raymond has just come out of the closet.'

'Oh, and remember your promise,' she said.

I never forget my promises, I thought, *someday soon to her, I am going to have to make the biggest promise of my life.*

Friday came, Saturday came and went and I picked up Joe and Molly in one of the zoo vans from their bungalow late that Sunday morning.

'Morning, my luvver, called Molly through the kitchen window, 'we're ready, just coming, come on, Joe.'

They got in the car. 'Hi Ben, you drive, I'll navigate,' said Joe.

The actual edge of the moor is rather difficult to define but there is a sort of hinterland consisting of deep valleys and small villages and hamlets before you get to the wilder bit.

The moor itself is about thirty miles wide and twenty deep and lies quite centrally in the county. It only took about twenty minutes to get to the outlying area and then the climb up to and onto the moor itself.

Some call it barren but it has a stark beauty that changes subtly in different lights. The roads are narrow and clogged in the summer months with tourists but this time of the year in autumn it is much quieter.

The village we wanted was on the western side of the moor, so we had to cut across the southern part to get to it.

'Go left here, then take the next left, first right and we should see the cottage at the end of the street. Hard to get lost here. One-horse town,' he joked. We arrived at very nice double-fronted thatched cottage with an evidently proud owner judging by the garden and its condition.

'There he is in the garden, the Professor,' said Molly.

Here was the real version of a professor caricature I always imagined.

Tweedy jacket, knitted tie, frayed shirt, brogue shoes of doubtful ancestry and the obligatory pair of totally shapeless brown cord trousers. The Professor, himself was of medium height, stooped, no doubt from too much library research and peering at me over a pair of tortoiseshell half glasses with surprisingly blue alert eyes. The glasses, of course, had one arm held together with sticking plaster.

We got out of the van and he opened the small garden gate for us.

'Welcome,' he said, 'to my home. This must be Ben. I have heard a lot about you, not all good, but then you wouldn't be interesting then, would you?'

'I've seen you at the zoo, sir,' I said.

'You probably have, I go there a lot.'

'Ben, this is Professor Lofthouse,' said Molly, 'Professor of social anthropology and my great uncle.'

'Retired, alas, and also this young ladies godfather, meant to be in charge of her religious and moral guidance. Didn't do a very good job,' he said, looking at Joe.

'That's sorted out, he is going to marry me,' said Molly.

Joe's jaw hit the floor. 'What, when?' he stuttered.

'To me, soon, you promised.'

'Got to give up drinking,' muttered Joe, 'see what happens, Ben. Warning bells should be ringing.'

'Got it, Joe.'

'Come inside and make yourself comfortable. I'll make us some coffee,' said the Professor.

We walked straight into a cosy living room with low beamed ceiling and a very old open fireplace. The room was overcrowded with furniture and on every surface, books. Books on shelves mostly askew, books on the tables, books on the chairs even books on the floor.

'Sorry about the mess,' said the Professor, entering with a tray, 'live on my own so no one to tell me off since my wife passed away. There's a coffee table under those books somewhere,' he joked, 'if you could clear it off, it would save me balancing it on top of this lot.'

'Now,' he said, 'if you are sitting comfortably, I'll begin, sorry, my little joke.

'Let me start with my background and then I will give you what I know or more accurately what I think I know.

'I was actually born in this village, not in this cottage, but in one down the road just like it, spent all my working life in academia first at Cambridge doing my degrees then at Durham where I lectured then finally back to my old college at Cambridge where I finally gained my professorship. Now, I am retired as I mentioned but do a lot of reading and research of a sort. My subject is social anthropology. I assume you know what that is, Ben.

'You must never make the mistake of believing that senior academics like myself know what they are talking about. We just have to sound like we do. Impresses the students you know. My subject is particularly difficult as it is part objective and part subjective. Some aspects can be tested and some cannot. This is one that cannot which is probably why I find it so fascinating.

'Let me start at the beginning. If I am repeating some of what Joe and Molly have told you, then I apologise but it is important for me to try and get this into some order and context.

'I understand you have spent a lot of time on the moor. It is a unique place with its rock outcrops, deep wooded valleys, bogs and marshes. Despite all this and the obvious hardship of living on the moor, it was once highly populated. Theories are that this was due to its height making it easier to defend and its distance from the sea making it unlikely to be invaded by raiders.

'Good workable theories, but there is something else here that might have attracted them and I will tell you who "they" were later in this story. The moor is crisscrossed with ley line, lines of natural energy. Then there are strange magnetic forces and if you have ever used a compass on certain parts of the moor, you will see that they just will not give a correct reading or the needle spins around. There is the radioactivity that permeates from the granite again naturally and finally the gases which emanate from the ground.

'The two last items are so virulent that it is now part of the building codes around here to test and design for screening and venting under buildings.

'After the original people came and settled here and died out, centuries went by until the 18th and 19th centuries when mining communities sprang up on and around the moor. They in turn due to industrialisation became abandoned and you can still see the signs of the old villages and hamlets if you know where to look.

'But let us go back to the original people whom I believe were Celts. The Celts moved westwards across Europe probably driven out by invaders from the east and it is believed and settled in Western Europe and what we now know as the United Kingdom. The Celts, in history, have been much maligned and almost classed as barbarians. Certainly, they were not Christian but worshipped earthly deities which almost certainly tainted their reputation.

'As time goes by, we are finding that the Celts were a highly developed culture with talented and skilled craftsmen. They had a huge respect for the land and let's call it Mother Earth. They had empathy with spiritual matters and the animals that lived with and around them.

'Just before the beginning of the first century, the Romans invaded and began to systematically wipe out any opposition. As their supply lines to the North and West got longer and more difficult, they finally came to the conclusion that their conquests would not serve any great purpose so these extremities were left alone. The wall, Hadrian's wall, was finally built in the North to keep out the Picts. The Celts, or those that survived, were pushed further South and West ending up mainly in Cornwall and Wales.

'This is where the synergy comes from in culture and language between those areas even including Brittany. Breton as a language is akin to Cornish which in turn has a relationship with Welsh. As these communities were separated, it was only natural that the original language root would develop differently. The Bretons, Cornish and Welsh have similar cultures and old religions, the latter being more visible with the Druids and Eisteddfod Festival. That festival alone echoes the cultural importance that then Celts gave to poetry, singing and dancing as a way to celebrate life forces and life itself.

'Now we come to some supposition on my part based on little or no evidence but research gained through what little information there is available.

'There is evidence on the moor of stone huts, so archaeologists tell me of belonging to an older civilisation. My assumption is that they have been the original settlers who were then joined by the Celtic invaders and assimilated with them.

'These we call here the "Old People" as we cannot categorise them. People here know them as the Feyr. They were fair-haired unlike the Celts who were darker. I do not know where their name comes from as it looks like some form of the Norse languages. Maybe it is derived from the faries or faeries. Who knows?

'What is interesting is that it is said that some of these people were endowed with special powers which they got from the earth and due to the culture of the Celts these special people were much prized and protected by the community.

'In time, the Celts and the old people were as one and then much later invasion of Anglo-Saxon farmers and later century miners settled in the area and gradually the old ways of living and the culture died out.

'I hope I am not boring you, Ben, I do rattle on a bit sometimes.'

'No, it is fascinating,' I said, 'please continue.'

'When I say that the old ways have died out, that is not quite true, as there is still evidence of some of the old ways even if their true meaning and purpose have been lost. We then see where some of the old ways have been integrated into

139

our modern culture and we just take them at face value. Christmas holly and mistletoe, maypoles, Morris dancers etc., etc.

'Even here, on the moor, there was a time, and not that long ago, when local farmers would chase around the moor on the night of the summer solstice looking to break up witches covens who were attracted to the remote disused chapel remains because they are the necessary consecrated ground.

'Where does legend end and reality begin? Perhaps all reality has a root in legend and the two are intertwined.

'Maybe then, as well, some of these old powers have been handed down and I think Joe and Molly have already mentioned the so-called psychic abilities to you of telekinesis, remote viewing; telepathy and more.

'So, where does this all take us and how does it relate to this young boy that you have found or has found you. Let us look at the factors we know about.

'He is about twelve or thirteen years old according to his medical examination but no one can find any trace of who he is or where he came from.

'He cannot or will not speak but appears to be able to communicate with animals in sounds some of which are beyond our hearing range. You believe this may be some form of language. I don't.

'He has no name other than the one you gave him. He understands language and has started to read some words which Joe and Molly are teaching him. He seems very bright and learns very quickly.

'He is well-behaved and compliant except where he is separated from those he trusts.

'Now I am going to switch on the scientific and more objective part of my brain and tell you what I conclude from all this. Bear in mind it is a theory and I might be completely wrong.

'First, I do not believe that this boy is some long lost "throwback" to an ancient people. The chances of him living to this age on the moor without being seen is quite ridiculous.

The next idea that he could have been orphaned when his parents or guardians were killed is also patently foolish as their names and his would almost certainly have come to light.

'My inference is that his family have either thrown him out as they could no longer deal with the lad or he has run away on his own volition due to some domestic problem and his parents or guardians are too embarrassed to say anything or glad to see the back of him.

'So, what about his so called powers?

'Let me turn your attention to some of these characteristics of this case and see if we can fit them in somewhere.

'You are all aware that there are people who have unusual skills and these appear through autism. The more highly developed are savants.

'I believe that we have many sense and skills, call them powers if you wish, which have been lying dormant and we know that there is a large part of our brain which is active but serve no known purposes. Some of these appear in people and some can be developed. Many of us can dowse for example and the more you practise, the better you get. Maybe it is not practise in itself but a coming together of some of the earth forces that helps to open up part of our dormant consciousness.

'What is odd about autism is that many sufferers seem to excel in some ways but lose normal abilities in doing so. I can give you examples of total visual recall, past life memory, photographic memory, the list goes on.

'Could it be that we have a recessive chromosome that has been passed down to us through our genes and pops us, excuse the phrase, in certain places and in certain people. This makes them special to us and historically feared by the unenlightened.

'Could it be that this boy is one of them and has the power to talk to animals? Just a theory, but I cannot think of a better one. I will leave these thoughts with you.

'Wow, it all fits,' I exclaimed, 'thank you for that, but what do we do about it?'

'Frankly, I do not have a clue,' said the Professor, 'but if I am right, you must protect and cherish this child just as I believe the ancients did.'

'Would you like to meet him?' I said.

'I already have, one day at the zoo. When Molly told me about him, I made it my business to seek him out. He was having a two-way conversation with some little monkeys which I think were Golden Tamarins. He did not know I was there but you were right. He has a very rare and precious gift.

'Well, I would offer you some refreshment but I cannot come close to competing with Molly's catering skills. I am now an old man and all this has quite tired me out so if you don't mind me being rude, I am going off for my afternoon *siesta*. You are welcome to stay.'

'Thanks, Uncle,' said Molly, 'we have left a friend in charge of him and given his single-mindedness, she will probably have her hands full or he has gone off somewhere. Found him in with the raccoons the other day when he was meant to be helping out one of the assistant keepers so not sure what we will find when we get back.'

Chapter 11
Winds of Change

The following day, it was back to work and having had a busy morning was now ensconced at our table with Joe, Molly and Cecilia. I had completely forgotten about Spencer when suddenly he appeared around the corner giving me no time to hide.

'Someone's been a busy boy,' said Molly.

'Bloody hell,' I exclaimed.

'Excuse me,' I said in a very authoritarian voice and pretending that I didn't recognise him, 'can I help you and by the way, why are you wearing Mr Wilks' zoo uniform?'

'It's me,' replied Spencer.

'Well, I have to admit you do look a bit like him, but no, it can't be.'

'It is me, really,' said Spencer, 'I took your advice and made some changes.'

'Stop teasing him, Ben, you can see he's trying really hard. Must have been very difficult for him,' said Cecilia.

'OK, now I look at you again, I can see. New hairstyle, new glasses and it even looks like you filed a bit off your pointy nose,' I said.

'Ben,' snapped Cecilia, 'stop now.'

'Spencer, we are very proud of you. You are a new man. Marjorie is going to freak out when she sees you. You are probably going to get ravished in the bushes.'

'Do you think so?' Spencer was looking none too confidant. 'She's coming here this afternoon, in fact in twenty minutes and I am going off to meet her at the main gate.' He rushed off.

'I have got to see this,' said Joe, 'I think a longer lunch break is totally in order.'

Nearly half an hour later, Cecilia, who had been designated as look out, came scampering back and quickly slid onto the picnic bench. 'For goodness sake, don't laugh, but we have another makeover coming this way.'

Around the corner came Spencer and Marjorie heading straight for us both with arms crossed behind their own backs. *Not the best body language,* I thought.

'Hello Marjorie,' said Cecilia, 'what a nice surprise. Are you on official business or is this your day off? Wow, you do look nice, what have you done to yourself. You and Spencer look like two shiny bright new people.'

Her lank, dark hair was slightly bobbed and had obviously had some sort of colour rinse to soften her dark hair. It actually moved when she did instead of giving the previous effect of being plastered to her head. New rimless glasses so she did not have to peer over the top and even makeup.

'Hello, everyone, bit of both, I need to have a private word with Joe and Molly and then I need to see Larry. I thought it was time I treated myself,' she said, 'tossing her new hairdo. Where is he by the way?'

'He's helping to clean out the macaws but I will fetch him if you like,' I said.

'No, I will speak to Joe and Molly first, then I will go and find him. Spencer, will you take me there afterwards?' Spencer nodded.

'We'll go to the office, if that's all right with you, Marjorie,' said Joe, 'follow us.'

The three of them went off and Spencer came and sat opposite Cecilia and me on the picnic table. He was highly excited.

'Did you see her, isn't she fantastic?' spluttered Spencer. 'I am really keen on her. What do you think I should do next?'

Cecilia gave me a warning stare and a slight shake of her head. 'Spencer,' she said, 'you two have been out several times and you have probably not yet got to first base.'

'He's probably still in the changing room,' I said interrupting her and getting a withering look in return.

'There is a moment in any budding relationship when someone has to take the initiative. In our case, it was me... Don't interrupt again, Ben, this is important,' she said, as I immediately opened and closed my mouth like a goldfish, 'she has obviously gone to a lot of trouble for you, Spencer, and this had nothing to do with her meeting with the other two. So, now, after they have finished, you need to take her to a nice private place away from visitors and staff and tell her how you feel.'

'But what happens if it doesn't work and she may never speak to me again,' he exclaimed close to tears.

'I don't think that is going to happen for a minute. I am a woman and I can read the signals. Now when you ask her to go with you, hold out your arm and hopefully she will take it, then escort her to somewhere nearby. If on the way your hand happens to slip into hers, then better still. Now when you are alone, hold both her hands, look into her eyes and tell her.'

'What should I say?'

'You could say something like, Marjorie, we have been seeing quite a lot of each time I can't wait for the next time. I like you very much and I would like us to have a wonderful relationship as we have so much in common.

'Now the words are very important, Spencer, and you must stop fidgeting and concentrate. The word "wonderful" is important and if you miss this out, it may sound like you are trying to proposition her and have your wicked way without the proper commitment. Now, I think you should practise this on me a couple of times.'

'Thanks, so much, Cecilia, you don't know what this means to me.'

'I'm going to leave you to it,' I said, 'going to make sure Larry is where he is meant to be.'

An hour later, I got back to the restaurant. Larry had not been where he was meant to be and I finally found him with the two Okapi at the furthermost part of their enclosure, and then I only spotted him because he had left his jacket on the fence by the main path. 'Come on, Larry, I want you back with the macaws as Ms Hoare is coming to see you and she isn't going to tramp all around the zoo looking for you.'

I got the usual cheery wave showing he had understood and I returned to the restaurant to find Joe and Molly returned; Cecilia with her head in her hands and Spencer gone.

'Spencer has gone to meet Marjorie and then they are heading for the parrots. I have had a devil of a job coaching Spencer so I give it a fifty, fifty chance of it succeeding even if he doesn't screw it up. 'But, enough about them, Joe and Molly have news.'

'We have got it,' said Joe, unable to contain his excitement, 'the papers. Marjorie brought them and it's all official. We are now his legal foster parents. At last!'

'There are some issues to sort out though,' said Molly, trying hard not to bubble over herself. 'We have to sort out a surname so he can have a health card and of course, he must have a proper birth date and then there is the schooling issue. The surname is not a problem; he can have Joe's so he will become Larry Bennett. For the birthday, we will have to rely on the doctor and say he is twelve years old and was born on April 28. The schooling bit gives me real concern, as I cannot see Larry being put into a normal school. He would get bullied because he is different and would end up in some institution for the disabled.

'So, we have talked about a compromise. Home schooling and this is where you two come into it as well. In fact, it was Marjorie who suggested this and I am beginning to like her more and more because in that stern exterior, I think there is a very nice caring person.'

'And, she doesn't want the hassle of sorting out his problems in a day school,' I said.

'Very cynical, Ben, not helping. I think we need to give Marjorie the benefit of the doubt. She has gone out on a limb on this one for us,' said Joe.

'What we have in mind is that Marjorie will tell us where to purchase the school curriculum for a twelve year old and we will spend two hours each evening taking him through it. Apparently, we will have to fill out a logbook and be ready for the school's inspector at any time. Now, you Ben, will be in charge of his education during the day. This does not mean that you have to do all of it yourself but you can delegate some of it. Cecilia will help, my lovely, won't you? Then Freddy will also do some stuff like biology. Somehow, we will get through it. What do you think?'

'Great idea, you two must be thrilled,' I said, 'it's taken long enough.'

'Remember though,' said Joe, 'this is a team effort. In reality, he does not belong to Molly and me, he belongs to all of us and belongs to no one. We are his guardians, not his custodians. We have a precious human being to protect. There will be times when things are going to go wrong; when people point him out as being something different. People will both love him and fear him for that reason alone. We must be on our guards.'

'Now, I know this sounds weird,' said Cecilia, 'but I want to see how those two lovebirds get on after all my coaching, so I am going to find out where they are and hopefully they will be finishing with Larry soonest.'

We walked quickly up the hill from the restaurant, hand in hand, then slowing down as we approached our destination, stopping on the way each time we saw or heard someone behind bushes, building equipment or whatever would give us cover. It was some time before Spencer and Marjorie emerged and we were nearly caught out as they had come from a completely different direction from where we thought they had been.

Some words were exchanged which we could not catch and then sure enough, according to plan, Spencer held out his crooked arm and Marjorie took it with a smile. 'So far, so good,' whispered Cecilia.

'What is,' said a quiet voice, Joe and Molly had been following us, 'you didn't think we were going to miss out on this, did you?'

'Stop whispering so loudly, they're going to hear you. I know where they are heading,' said Cecilia, 'I did mention a nice quiet grove of trees behind the isolation enclosures where they could have some privacy. Larry was obviously a better student than I gave him credit for. Now, Spencer, try and hold her hand,' she urged silently.

'We can cut them off; there is an alley on the other side and some bushes where it come out into the grove. Quick and quietly,' I said.

We hustled around the buildings, took a right turn down the alley and emerged behind the bushes just as Spencer and Marjorie entered the grove, still not holding hands. There was not enough room under one bush for the four of us so we ended up under a sprawling magnolia tree and the other two behind their own non-descript bush next to us.

Spencer was looking like he was trying to hold himself together. 'Lose the scowl, Spencer,' I whispered, 'you are going to scare her to death.'

'He's trying to concentrate,' whispered back Cecilia, 'I think I may have overdone it a bit and given him too much to think about. No, look, he's taken her two hands in his like I told him to. Now, look into her eyes and talk to her. Damn, I can't hear a thing.'

The next few minutes were a piece of theatre. Spencer talking earnestly to Marjorie while still holding her hands but not looking into her eyes but staring off to one side at the ground when suddenly...

It is very easy to underestimate people and this time, it was a usually staid Marjorie who took the initiative. She put her hand gently across his mouth, presumably to stem the flow, then cupped his ears in her hands and went for the big smacker.

Spencer rocked back on his heels and it was only her tight grip on either side of his head that prevented him from keeling over.

'For a woman with such thin lips she really has got a huge mouth,' I said softly in awe, 'looks like she has his mouth and nose in one. He must be breathing through his ears that is, if he is still alive. She reminds me of one of those sink plungers.'

'Will you shut up?' whispered Molly. 'This is fun, don't spoil it.'

148

'Now she looks as though she is trying to suck his nasal membranes. What we are seeing here folks, is a complete by-pass of puberty and a suicidal dive into the netherworld of pure lust. Bloody glad I had lunch because I wouldn't want to watch this on an empty stomach. I'm off, you two coming?'

'No, we're not for the moment,' whispered Molly, 'see you later.'

'What are you two up to in there?'

The bushes parted and Joe's face appeared. 'Sod off, there's a good lad,' he said.

We very quietly backed out of our hiding place feeling like a pair of voyeurs and started off back down the hill past the Administration when who should appear but Walt and Mabel with Larry between them.

'Heard the news,' said Walt, 'delighted with the outcome and as you can see, Mabel has managed to get a present for him from all of us to honour the occasion. Couldn't get the badge in time but as you can see, a smart new recruit.

I had not noticed at first but now Larry was wearing a zoo uniform complete with working boots, shirt, tie and dungarees. He was holding a pair of rubber boots in a plastic bag in one hand and a woolly hat with the zoo badge on it in the other. He was looking very pleased with himself.

'So, without further ado,' said Walt, 'I would formally welcome our newest member of staff Master Larry Bennett. So, shake hands with me Master Bennett and with Mabel. OK, so you would rather kiss her. Can't blame you. Oh! And you want to kiss me as well. This is a first.'

'Have you seen Spencer? We should let him in on this before anyone else finds out. Protocol, you know.'

'He has his hands full at the moment, but I will let him know you want to see him as soon as he is finished, Mr Whitlam.'

'What's he up to, Ben?'

'Some sort of mating problem, question of compatibility, bye for now.'

The following morning started quietly with my usual rounds. Suddenly, my phone rang. 'Quick, come to the gorillas,' a voice said which I did not recognise.

I ran, well sort of shuffled up to the primate area and as I got close, I was more than aware of an awful lot of people going the same way amid much excitement. By the time I got there, they were three deep at the enclosure screens so I went around the back to be met by Billy, one of my underlings who worked in the primate area.

'Thank God, you came, I don't know what to do,' cried Billy, 'he's in there and I don't know what to do.'

'Right, first calm down, Billy. Now who is in there and how did he get in?'

'It's Larry, the boy, he must have gone in by the inside enclosure and he's in there with them all. If I go near them to try to get him out, they might get defensive and hurt him.'

That's a relief, it's Larry so I am not going to get worried, I thought, Billy has a point though, he may be OK but the gorillas are more likely to defend him than anything else.

'Where's Rwanda, Billy?'

'You had better look for yourself but go around through the inside enclosure because you can always close the outer door if they rush you. You won't be able to get around the front, too many people.'

Now gorillas are amazing creatures but you have to be very careful. They live in a tight family group and the head, in this case Rwanda is a silver back male probably weighing over 400 lbs and they are surprisingly quick. In there with him are two females, his harem Emily and Sylvia plus a three-year-old youngster called Boo. As Rwanda is the boss, his "wives" are named after the Pankhurst sisters, as they never get to vote.

Gorillas have to respect the hierarchy so when you approach one, it is better to be low and humble. Do not make eye contact and definitely do not mess with the wives.

I went through the huge inner enclosure followed by Billy and peered through the open outer sliding door. Amidst the noise from the gathering throng, there was Larry fast asleep next to Rwanda. His left arm was over Rwanda's chest and close next to him was one of the females with Boo on her lap. What was even funnier was Rwanda was gently picking through Larry's hair and every now and then would examine a small piece of something and put it in his mouth.

I couldn't help but burst out laughing. Billy looked at me as though I was mad. 'What are you going to do?' he said.

'Nothing,' I laughed again, 'he is perfectly safe. Now look again and tell me what you see from a behaviour point of view, you being the primate keeper.'

Billy looked and looked again. 'Blimey, Rwanda is cleaning him and this is a ritual where the juniors show their obeisance to the head of the family by grooming. In the wild, they are searching for fleas or lice.'

'Correct, Billy, except in this case he is not only grooming Larry, I suspect for skin flakes rather than fleas or lice, but also look at what Sylvia is doing.'

'She's not doing anything, just sitting there.'

'And what do you make of that, Mr Expert?'

'The alpha male would not usually let any stranger near one of his wives and if one tried, he would be warned off and if persisted would likely be killed by the silverback.'

'Correct again, Billy, so what is your conclusion?'

'Well, I can only think that the boy has been accepted as a part of the family and is recognised as being too young and immature to be a threat to Rwanda.'

'So what would you do?'

'I have no idea, best to leave them alone, I guess. If we go in there, we may upset things but it's a bit difficult just doing nothing.'

'My thought exactly, the main problem is the visitors gawping. This is going to take a lot of explaining. If we do one thing, and you are right, someone might get hurt. If we do nothing, we look as though we are not trying. Tricky one.'

'What's going on?' Joe had arrived and we moved aside so he could see the scene for himself. 'I knew something like this would happen one day, what was he meant to be doing?'

'The problem is, Joe,' I said, 'that because he is a minor, he is technically only allowed to work so many hours in a week so we have to pretend that some of the time he is on educational tasks. The reality is, I give him a worksheet or to one of the keepers and after he finishes, he can do what he likes. He keeps a book or two in his bag so if someone asks any awkward questions, he can pretend he is studying.'

'Quick, look,' said Joe suddenly, as I had just finished, Boo had crawled on to his lap and woken him up. I saw his eyes open.

Billy and I looked through the plate glass next to the open door and sure enough, Larry's eyes were open. He stretched out his arms and looked around with surprise first at the noisy visitors with their cameras flashing and then around the enclosure finally to the three of us.

A cheery wave and then he just settled back down and closed his eyes. Rwanda stroked his face, pushed Boo off his lap and replaced his arm around Larry's shoulder.

'Let's get out of here and leave them but we need to think up something quickly. I smell trouble,' said Joe, 'best if you leave the outer door open. Billy, you stay there while we get out in case they rush the door then you follow.'

The three of us got outside. 'What's your plan for this one, Ben?' asked Joe.

'I have an idea, but I don't think it will stand examination by someone who knows about gorillas,' I replied. 'First, Billy, you go around the path as people are going to ask you questions if you go around the front. You stand out a mile in your zoo outfit and a lot of this mob has already seen you in the gorilla enclosure. Do not talk to anyone. Is that very clear?'

Billy did as I asked and took the private back maintenance path away from the primate area while we prepared to face the crowd who now numbered probably in excess of a hundred people.

The sight of us set off a prolonged barrage of questions and yet more camera flashes.

You could imagine the questions from peals of delight to recriminations to a range of stupid suggestions and comments.

'Are you just going to leave him in there?'

'Won't they eat him?'

'Why don't you just go in there and drag him out?'

'Don't you have a gun thing to knock the big one out?'

'Sorry, ladies and gentlemen,' I shouted, 'no questions now, just move quietly away because we mustn't scare the animals or they might get upset or even angry.'

Three more keepers had arrived, no doubt informed by Billy to see if they could help. I asked them to help to politely usher people away. They did not want to go but eventually and very reluctantly, they trooped off, some to a "safe" distance and others to continue their tour of the zoo.

One stalwart approached us. 'Got a phone call and just got here,' said the man, 'my name is John Lincoln and I'm from the local paper.' He pulled out his press card with a flourish thinking that this would impress us and give him a private passport to this event.

'I believe you were asked to move back,' said Joe with authority, 'we asked everyone to leave them alone and that includes you. Don't argue, you might be putting the boy at risk, so please move back.'

We walked off, he followed. This one was made of sterner stuff no doubt weaned by many rejections and worse.

'Look, I have a job and a duty to the public,' he said, 'this is a great news story and I want the scoop, so if you don't tell me, I am going to have to make something up or my editor will be very upset and you wouldn't want to upset my editor. Nasty temper.'

'I don't give a rat's ass about you or your editor,' shouted Joe, 'and if you try and threaten us, Ben here will be introducing you to our colony of baboons and you can show them your press card and tell them about your editor.'

Give this guy his due, he took this blast without flinching and then tried his well-rehearsed wheedling.

'Sorry, I just got a bit carried away,' he wheedled, 'I know you blokes have a job to do and are in a bit of a pickle but I do need something for our readers. Look at it this way, a good story is going to put this zoo on the map. Think of the increased income, the popularity, won't your Board be pleased. Now it's happened you can't hush it up, so make the best of it. What do you say?'

Joe and I looked at each other and he shrugged, raised one eyebrow at me in silent acknowledgement and said, 'Ben, tell him.'

'You make a valid point and we don't want any adverse publicity, so we will give you a story which I hope will please your readers and your editor for that matter. Have you taken any photos? If not, just come back with me and take some quickly before anyone sees you and takes it as an invite to return.' He walked over to the enclosure with me, adjusted his camera and took some pictures while I waited. Larry was still fast asleep.

Joe had by now disappeared, no doubt to personally report to Walt before someone else did leaving me with the reporter.

'Let me start at the beginning,' I said, 'The boy you see in there is an orphan whose parents were killed by poachers in Rwanda. He grew up with gorillas and learned their ways. They do not see him as a threat so they accept him as one of them. After his parents were killed, he accompanied Emily, one of the females, whom he grew up with and that helped the big male to accept him as well. Since they have been here, Sylvia and her son have also got used to him. What you have seen today is an everyday event except on this occasion he was up all night helping with a wounded spider monkey and simply fell asleep. Not much of a story I'm afraid.'

'Not much of a story!' exclaimed the reporter, 'You must be joking. This is front-page stuff. People just love stories about animals. It's going to be great. My editor is going to be so pleased.'

'I have been straight with you; now I want two things in return. Can you promise me that you are not going to do the tabloid thing and sensationalise this thing to pieces and that you are not going to try and interview the boy?'

'I can promise you the world but in the end, it will be up to my editor. They are all powerful you know and what they decide goes. He will definitely want me to interview the boy.'

'Well, you can tell him that it will do him no good.'

'Why's that?'

'The boy cannot talk, the trauma of his parents' death was too much and he has lost that ability,' I lied, 'but I will tell you what, you can have an exclusive as long as you agree to these points or you will never set foot in this zoo again.'

'I already have a story and photos so it is no good trying to pressure me like that,' he said petulantly.

'I will have to leave it to your own conscience then,' I said.

'I am a reporter, we are a specially chosen race without one,' he replied.

'Goodbye, Mr Lincoln.'

'Cheerio,' he replied.

The following day, I waited with bated breath for the newspapers to appear. The dailies came but the local paper was delayed. Sure enough, the front page had a picture of Larry cosily asleep between the gorillas. Thankfully, no crass headlines or captions and it had been written more as a curio-type story than a sensational one. Mr Lincoln, or whoever had written it, had used my story verbatim.

'You did well there,' said Walt, 'could have got really nasty. Oh, nearly forgot, could you call Ms Hoare. She wants to speak to you. Here is her number. Call her now.'

I dialled her private number at her office. 'Good morning, I mean afternoon, Marjorie, it's Ben, understand you wanted a word.'

'Yes, Ben, I understand that you have found out where Larry came from, his parents being killed by poachers and all that.'

'I have a confession, Marjorie, that was not true, I said that to the reporter who was being a nuisance to try and avoid a much more difficult explanation.'

'I see,' she said, 'I think you had better explain to me then why you let a twelve-year-old boy that I personally pushed through the system to be in your care happens to end up asleep with some very powerful and potentially dangerous animals.'

'I see your point,' Marjorie, but it's not quite like that.'

'Well, you had better come up with something very quickly because orders can be revoked and I am not happy.'

'This is not good over the phone, Marjorie, how about we meet and discuss this properly?' I pleaded.

There was a pause and then Marjorie said with a very severe sounding voice. 'Tomorrow I want you, the foster parents, your girlfriend and the boy to meet me at the zoo at ten o'clock in the morning and we will go through this.'

'Thanks, Marjorie, see you tomorrow.'

Trouble, I thought, *time to gather the others.*

Twenty minutes later, four of us had gathered at the restaurant and I had filled them in about the situation.

'Ben, what were you thinking of?' said Molly, 'You have jeopardised everything.'

'That's not very fair, I can't watch him every minute of the day. He was up with Freddy all night helping him and he just fell asleep. Let's be honest, you two don't know where he is all night when he's not with you. I know what you are going to say, he's safe on Gibbon Island.'

'Yes, not only that, but he is safely out of sight and even if he weren't, there are no visitors around,' said Molly.

'OK, I screwed up and I have been awake half the night thinking about it, but I have a plan and hopefully it will work.'

'Come on then, let's hear it,' said Cecilia.

'We are going to invite Marjorie to the island and introduce her to the gibbons through Larry.'

'Am I thinking what you are thinking, Ben,' said Cecilia.

'What's he thinking?' said Molly.

'Think I know,' said Joe, 'you think that Larry is going to work his magic on her and hopefully she will understand that he is absolutely safe with the animals.'

'Hole in one,' Joe.

'I get it,' said Molly, 'I can see this working. I have not experienced this feeling you were talking about but I have enough faith in you and belief in Larry to accept it.'

So, we waited for the following day with trepidation.

At nine forty five the following morning, Marjorie appeared with Spencer in tow.

'What's going on, Ben? Marjorie asked me to be in on this. In on what?'

'You'll see, Spencer, all will be revealed.' *I hope,* I thought.

'Are you all here?' said Marjorie.

'I thought it would be a good idea if we went to Larry's favourite place for our chat,' I said.

'And where is that, may I ask?' said Marjorie.

'On the island,' I said.

'Well, I won't have anyone say I'm not flexible,' she replied, 'let's go.'

The usual route was taken although it took three trips across because the boat would only take three people at a time with one of those rowing of course, so it was all good while before we were all properly assembled on the island. The gibbons had retreated to the trees and were hooting their soft warning sounds at the sight of strangers in their home.

'It's very pleasant here,' said Marjorie, looking around, 'I don't suppose these monkeys are dangerous?'

'They will give you a good bite if they don't like you,' I told her playing their behaviour up a bit. 'At the moment, they are up in the trees trying to work out what is going on but believe me there are a lot of them.'

'How many?' Marjorie asked, looking around nervously.

'There are a dozen of them, but now we are going to show you the real reason we have brought you here and hopefully you will see,' I said, 'let's all sit down on these logs. Larry will you call them please.'

Larry stood up, smiled at Marjorie, cupped his hands to his mouth and let out a strange noise which seemed to start in his chest and emerge as a rumbling whistle through his mouth. A pause, then nothing happened. He held up his hand in a gesture which could have meant quiet or wait. I think it was wait.

Two minutes later, a small black face appeared on the branch above him. The gibbon grabbed hold of the branch between his legs and gently swung down on top of Larry's head. The gibbon slid downwards until his arms were around Larry's neck and his legs wrapped around his waist. Then the next one appeared, then the next. Suddenly, there were five of them, then three more and soon all twelve were there either on the branch above, on Larry or the more adventurous ones sitting on the log or ground next to him.

'He certainly has them tamed,' she said, 'they're very cute.'

'They don't behave like this with just anyone,' said Spencer, 'I have watched Larry very carefully over the past months since he has been here, and I have no doubt that he has a special relationship with these animals.'

Thank you, Spencer, I thought, *you have just joined the human race. That little speech has set the scene nicely.*

'Larry, would you like to introduce your pals to Marjorie, please.'

'Does that mean I have to hold one?' she said, obviously in two minds about the prospect.

'Don't worry, Marjorie, it's quite safe, as long as you are with Larry. Not so much a question of you holding them but them hanging onto you. Hold Larry's hand and they will be reassured.' *I'm a crafty sod,* I thought.

Larry reached out his hand to Marjorie and he whispered something to the first gibbon who immediately detached itself and climbed aboard Marjorie.

'What a lovely creature,' she exclaimed, as the gibbon stared at her from a distance of six inches. 'You could almost feel what he is thinking. Is it a he or a she?'

'It's a she,' I said, 'this is Beth.'

'Hello, Beth,' said Marjorie, 'Oh! Here is another one who wants to say hello.' Within a few minutes, four more had climbed on her and two more were sitting on the ground at her feet. 'They're all different colours and sizes.'

'This is a variation on how many people you can get in a telephone box,' I joked, 'how many gibbons can you get on a Marjorie?'

'As many as you like,' said Marjorie, giggling, 'wish I could stay but this was a fleeting visit and I am already late. Can I come another time?'

'You can come any time you like, Marjorie,' said Joe, 'you are always welcome.'

We got everyone back on to the main shore and Marjorie turned to say goodbye. And to thank us.

'Marjorie before you go, can I ask you a question?'

'Yes, of course.'

'Do you understand?'

She paused for a few moments. 'Yes, I think I understand, but I do not know what I understand,' she answered cryptically. 'I'm glad Larry is safe and happy. Is that what you wanted to hear?'

'It will do fine,' I said.

She walked off arm in arm with Spencer.

'I think your plan worked, there, my luvver,' said Molly, 'lucky.'

'You know and I know luck had nothing to do with it.'

'It was magical,' said Cecilia, 'the change that came over her.'

'Something like that,' said Joe.

Chapter 12
Fame – A Two-Edged Sword

'Ben,' said John Lincoln on the telephone, 'we have a problem. You have been very straight with me and we are not having this conversation. My editor has syndicated the story.'

'What does that mean?'

'It means that the paper with the scoop sells the story to other newspapers. Smaller local newspapers make a lot of money doing this and it also saves the nationals sending their staff out, so it works financially both ways.'

'So what is the problem?'

'The problem is, Ben, that our newspaper has no control over what they do with the story. My editor chose to take a, let's say, a conservative line on the story. The nationals, especially the tabloids have a tendency to sensationalise things to make them racier and eye catching. So, just giving you a heads up on this. One last thing, if the nationals do run with it they usually want to do a follow up and you are likely to have some very pushy unwelcome visitors in the shape of reporters and photographers.'

'Thanks for that, John, we will have to be on our guard. I will tell Mr Whitlam. Thank you for that. Bye.'

On my way up to Walt's office, my phone rang. Not a number I recognised, so I just hit the cancel button and continued. My phone rang again and this time I did recognise Spencer's number.

'Hi Spencer, what's up?'

'You need to get to the rhino enclosure Ben, it's Larry. We don't want anyone seeing what he's up to.'

'What is he up to?'

'He is playing football with the baby rhino.'

'Who's winning?'

'Ben, this is serious,' spluttered Spencer.

'Where's mama rhino?'

'In there with them.'

'What position is she playing?'

'Ben,' shouted Spencer in exasperation, 'for goodness sake.'

'OK, I'm almost there. I can see you now, Spencer.' Spencer dashed up to me in a high dudgeon. 'What are we going to do?' he said.

We had given Monty the baby rhino a football some days previously and he spent most of his waking moments chasing the thing around the hard surfaced parts of his enclosure. Great sight because baby rhinos are an exact miniature copy of the adults but play like most other youngsters so it is very comical. He doesn't have a horn yet so he just pushes the ball around with his nose or occasionally his feet.

Mama rhino was standing watching very stoically apparently completely unmoved or threatened by the two of them. Papa rhino was behind some very stout separating bars and was watching the show without any expression. Every now and then, the ball would arrive below her feet and one of the other two would run over and nose or kick it out.

'What shall we do?' said Spencer.

'Get in there with them, make a game of it. Come on.'

'You must be joking if you think I am going to get in there with a full grown rhino. That little one could knock me off my feet. God knows what the big one will do.'

'Well, I am going just for five minutes. Just keep a look out.'

The baby rhino took us both on. Monty's idea of winning the ball was to simply charge through the person shielding it. So after a few tumbles and the rudiments of a passing game, Monty was starting to show signs of exhaustion which coincided with a warning shout from Spencer. A keeper with two of the rabble in tow was coming, so I motioned to Larry for us to get out fast.

'Hi guys,' said the keeper, 'just coming to feed and clean out the rhinos. Is Monty all right, why is he lying down like that?'

'We've been watching him playing with his football and he's been overdoing it a bit. He's just resting,' I replied.

Larry, Spencer and I walked away and Larry suddenly took Spencer's hand. 'You see, someone likes you Spencer.'

'Very funny. You know, I really like having him around,' said Spencer, 'I have never seen anyone have such a rapport with the animals. It's almost like he grew up with them all and watching him with the rhinos was astonishing. When you got in there as well, I was expecting trouble, I can tell you, but it seems that if one of us is with him, he is accepted and safe.'

Very perceptive, Spencer, I thought. *If we tell him what we think we know, it's going to blow his mind.*

'Marjorie thinks he's great, she told me,' he said, 'she wants to spend more time here with him and visit the island again.'

'Next time, we will get Larry to first introduce her to Raymond then to Blimp. That will really give her a thrill.'

'Not sure she is quite ready for that, Ben.'

'Have a little faith, Spencer. I'll have a bet with you that she is.'

'To be honest, Ben, there are so many weird things happening that nothing would surprise me anymore.'

You're getting there, Spencer, I thought. *Yes, you are getting there.*

We went our separate ways, Larry to the lake, me to the office and Spencer who knows where. I walked into the administration reception to be confronted with Mabel.

'Ben, have you had any strange phone calls this morning, there is someone trying to you. I spoke to him get through and I don't like his tone. He was asking questions about Larry and the gorillas.'

I told her what John Lincoln had told me and this looked as though it could be the forerunner of a news binge.

'He told me if I did not tell him something, they would print something anyway,' said Mabel, 'so I should cooperate.'

'I told him it was not my place to comment.'

'How did he get my telephone number?' I asked, assuming it was the same person who was trying to call me.

'I certainly didn't give him it,' she said.

'Not blaming you for one minute, Mabel.'

'Now I think about it, there was a man in here this morning that I have never seen before. He had a phone in his hand. Now I've got it, he must have taken a photo of the list of telephone numbers on the wall there. I wondered what he was doing. Has to be that. Sneaky git.'

'John Lincoln warned me that these guys were pushy and had a lot of underhand tricks. See you later.'

On my way down the hill to the restaurant, I got another call, this time from Joe. 'Have you had any strange phone calls or seen anyone around asking questions. Where are you?'

'Heading down to the restaurant. Be there in two minutes.'

'I'll meet you there.'

'Hi Ben, I think we have a problem. There is a guy snooping around. He has already spoken to one of the keepers, the lady in the shop, one lady on the gate and two of the Rabble. What do you know?'

I filled Joe in with what had gone on that morning. 'Joe, we can't hide him, so maybe we should take the bull by the horns and just confront him.'

'I don't trust those buggers,' said Joe.

'Nor do I but at the end of the day, they are going to print what they want. Where's Larry?'

'Where do you think? If you look closely, you can see the end of his boot sticking out over there so he should be safe but honestly, we can't shelter him forever.'

The phone rang. It was Mabel. 'This guy's back. He's here in the office. Will you come back here?'

'On our way, Mabel,' I replied.

During the four or five minute walk up the hill, we tried to formulate a plan and decided to stick to the original story. The problem was that the bigger newspapers, if that was indeed where he came from, had an awful lot more resources and our story may not stand up to professional scrutiny.

When we arrived at the office, Mabel greeted us with a roll upward of her eyes as if to say silently say "watch out".

'Good morning,' said the man, 'I'm from the Daily Sketch and here to do a story about this remarkable event. Here is my card. My name is Jake Freemont. What can you tell me?'

'Good morning, Mr Freemont,' said Joe menacingly, 'can we assume that it was you that has been trying to call us and was it you that took unauthorised photos of our private phone numbers because if it is, then you and I have got off to a very bad start.'

Now, being the size that Joe is, if he had said that, in that tone to anyone else, I would have expected them to be heading for the door rather rapidly but this guy was made of sterner stuff and probably had a skin a good deal thicker than one of our rhinos.

'Look,' he said with a leery grin, 'all's fair in love and war.'

'Well, this is neither love nor war, so enough of the clichés, what do you want?'

'A good story.'

'I don't think we can add anything more than what the local paper gleaned from us,' I said.

'I'm sure that's not true,' he replied, 'I've been in this game a long time and I can smell a good story. So let's level with each other.'

'Right,' said Joe, 'I don't like the way you have gone about this and I suppose the next thing you are going to say is "freedom of the press" and "only working in the public interest". Heard it all before so don't waste your breath. You ask us questions and we will answer those as we feel comfortable with. Go!'

'First question,' said the reporter, 'who is this boy?'

'He happens to be my foster child. He is twelve years old and his name is Larry. He is home-schooled because he cannot speak and spends the required number of hours working in the zoo under our supervision after which he has some further formal education with one of our staff. The rest you know.'

'I understand that his parents were killed by poachers and he arrived here with one of the gorillas. What were their names?'

'Even we do not know that,' said Joe, 'his parents were involved in the investigation into an international poaching ring and we have been told that they have to remain anonymous or other people involved in the operation might be prejudiced.'

Well done, Joe, I thought, *that sounded really good.* The reporter looked doubtful.

'Sounds a bit far-fetched to me,' he said. 'Where did you say this all happened?'

'I didn't,' replied Joe, 'I hope you will respect the security aspect of the situation.'

'Can I speak to the boy? Get another picture?'

'No, we have been advised by the doctor to keep him calm and to try and not remind him of the trauma he has been through. We hope that one day his voice may return. Until then, you may not speak to him. He is a minor. If you want to know anything, then come through the office and use the proper channels.'

'OK, if that is all I am going to get out of you, I will be on my way. Thanks.'

'One last thing,' said Joe, 'we use our phones here very sparingly. I do not appreciate you calling or bothering our staff. If this behaviour persists, I will have you banned from the zoo altogether. Just stand there, I'm going to take your photo just in case.'

After the reporter left, Joe decided it would be best if we informed Walt what was going on which we did some two hours later on his return from one of his frequent meetings. Walt in turn deemed it necessary to gather the department heads so that they in turn could be made aware of the situation and pass this on to their staff. We were all ordered not to talk to anyone but to refer any approaches to the office.

'Do you think that's it,' I said, 'silly question, there's going to be more to come.'

'Afraid so,' replied Joe.

The following morning, Mabel came running down to the restaurant where the five of us were having breakfast. 'Have you seen the newspapers?' she said, 'I have only got two but the story seems to be in all of them complete with the same picture of Larry lying between the gorillas.'

She laid the two newspapers out on the table and sure enough the headlines ran:

IS THIS THE NEW JUNIOR TARZAN

and

HAVE WE FOUND THE MISSING LINK

'The first one is a bit pathetic,' said Cecilia, 'but the other one is rather clever.'

We each read the articles which had very little to do with the truth but mainly consisted of speculation.

'More bad news,' said Mabel, 'the local TV station wants to be involved and have asked for an appointment. Mr Whitlam would like to see you all sometime this morning.'

'The flood gates are open,' said Molly despairingly.

'We need a plan,' said Joe.

'Run and hide,' said Cecilia.

'Let's go and see Walt. Larry, go and find Freddy and help him please this morning. You go with Cecilia to the preparation rooms and then help Emily with the animal food preparation.'

The three of us walked slowly up the hill with Mabel and arrived just in time to find Walt devouring the remains of his breakfast. Spencer was also there.

'I have shown them the newspapers as you asked,' reported Mabel.

'Let's go into the meeting room,' said Walt, 'and get comfortable. Right, now then, there is a way of dealing with the press but basically you are damned if you do and damned if you don't. If you refuse to tell them anything, it is potentially more damaging as they will make up something and make it as juicy as they can. If you do tell, them something then they will always want more. Luckily, I have had some experience in this. You have made a good start with the story you are spinning but do not for one-minute underestimate their perseverance. They have papers to sell, viewers to satisfy and they are not too worried how they do it.

'The TV is a little more responsible than the newspapers. The bit I fear most is their usual ploy of building something up then going on a crusade to knock it down. Our vulnerability lies not in the main story but the potential follow-ups. For example, they could say that we are unfit to look after a traumatised child which will lead on to questions about how this came about and put social services in the loop.

'They may talk about how a responsible zoo could allow a child in with dangerous animals.

'However, I have been thinking about this and will put my idea to you.

'Let us try and turn this around and take the initiative. Instead of sheltering Larry, let us throw him into the limelight so to speak. We know that Larry is not traumatised but they don't. We can say that his involvement with the animals is a carefully crafted strategy to help his recovery and we have invented a special position for him on our staff to help show live animals to our public in a safe and educational way of course under the tutelage of the lovely Cecilia.

'The other thing is of course, that handled properly this could help the zoo no end. Our numbers are down and cost up so we could do with some serious marketing and at no expense to the zoo.

'So in conclusion, this affair could be a two edged sword.'

'I see you with new eyes, Mr Whitlam,' I said.

'I could take that two ways, Ben, but knowing you, I will take it as a compliment,' said Walt. 'Right game plan.

'Let's leave the newspapers alone and concentrate on the television thing. Mabel, you set up a meeting with the TV Company for tomorrow.

'Joe, you have a word with Larry first then fill all the others in with what we are going to do. Ben, you have a chat with your girlfriend... No good looking like that, Ben, do you think I don't know what's going on. Good choice, but I digress.

'You need to formulate some plan with Cecilia to put the live animal demonstrations on a timetable. Not only should this include the, let's say, tamer ones in the visitor pavilion but we need to be a little more adventurous.

'How would you feel Joe and Ben if Larry was to actually go in with the gorillas, lions, tigers, and rhinos at certain times of the day just as we do now with, for example feeding times for certain animals. These have always been very popular.

'How about a ride with Larry on Elsie the elephant or one of the camels. No, camels, probably not, I don't trust those things. So the question is to you two. How much confidence do you have in the apparent empathy that Larry has with the animals for him not to be mauled or eaten in front of the great British public.'

'I think tiny steps to begin with Geoffrey,' said Joe, 'I think we should hang back on the elephant ride or getting bigger animals out of their enclosures for the time being until we see how it goes. Every now and then, we could organise a parade where certain ones come out but the public are kept back behind barricades.'

'Suppose you're right, Joe, I just had visions of Larry and Bling riding down the main concourse on Elsie watched by thousands of entry-paying people but I will reluctantly have to curb that ambition for the time being and listen to you.'

So, it all happened as planned. Larry was given a "junior" keeper costume complete with his name badge, which had been forgotten about before and a hat of course. A new schedule of animal feeding, educational talks and communing with the animals sessions were all set up with the accompanying literature and signage then Walt declared us ready for the press.

'Now the way we play this is to hold a press conference,' he said. 'I will speak to our advertising agency chums to organise it as they have the contacts and they will circulate an invitation to newspapers and magazines. I particularly want National Geographic there as they are recognised as being the best.

'Then after the press conference, we organise a tour with the TV producers to plan out a programme. Tell me when you think we are ready. Mabel is going to act on my behalf as co-ordinator.

'Don't forget to tell Marjorie what is going on, Spencer, she has been a great ally to us in all this. Don't blush, Spencer, it amazes me that you lot don't think I know what's going on. You and Marjorie, hey? Good for you.

Remember, I have eyes and ears everywhere.'

'Do I get a pay rise for this, Mr Whitlam?'

'Don't be silly, Mabel, you should relish the task and do this for nothing.'

'As if I have a choice,' said a rueful Mabel.

'That's the spirit, Mabel, knew I could rely on you. What is our status?'

'Well, Mr Whitlam, the temporary signs and blackboards are in place. We have handouts that we have created ourselves. They are just photocopies for now. The printers will deliver the proper ones next Tuesday but too late for your press conference so whenever you want to call it we are as ready as we can be.'

The following week, the press conference went really well. I was told to wear my clean uniform and to wear my hat which I had a lot of difficulty finding but finally turned up on the gatepost of the deer enclosure where I had left it several weeks earlier. It had suffered from a couple of storms and UV exposure and took a lot of work by Cecilia to regain its shape and some of its colour. Walt took one look at it and sighed.

There was a brief question session after the conference which was a bit awkward as the inevitable questions came up which were becoming increasingly difficult to field. However, we got through it, as the attendees were more anxious to see the result of the live action and the show we put on for them.

The newspapers, meanwhile, had gone strangely quiet. There were varying reports on the new initiatives and more pictures of Larry with the animals. Next came the reporter from the TV station who had been invited quite separately and there we were, the next day on local TV and a good report it was too.

Next came the professional stuff that Mabel had ordered being the signs and leaflets followed by visit from producers of the TV company who had decided to do a full, half hour feature programme to the delight of Walt.

The production crew arrived as a sort of forward search party. Not one or two but six of them. There was a producer, his assistant, a location planner, camera boss, scriptwriter and another person whom we never did find out what function he performed. May have driven the van for all I knew.

Clearly, TV planning was not a simple turn up with a camera crew, write a few lines and start filming. There was a lot of planning and preparation involved and there were several pre-visits to accommodate, schedules, timetables, refreshments etc.

The day was set for the filming and it was decided to close the zoo as we could not control visitors who would be wanting to prance around in front of the cameras or worse.

My observations on the vents of that day.

Walt has raised himself to superstar status complete with one of those shiny suits which made the camera crew very unhappy due to the glare.

Molly spent the day between fits of laughter dispensing tea and coffee to everyone.

Marjorie had appeared on the pretext of making sure that Larry was not being taken advantage of.

Larry complete with makeup thought it was a great joke but played his part like a real trouper and made sure all the animals behaved themselves.

Joe tried to hide but they found him in the Gents angrily declaring that he had a stomach issue and could not take part. The ruse didn't work which set Molly off again into helpless laughter.

I tried to hide but they sent Mabel to find me. I thought she was my friend but the power of the spotlight won and not only was makeup applied but I was forced to borrow Spencer's immaculate hat as mine was deemed to be totally unsatisfactory.

The cameras did not miss the lovely Cecilia and I got jealous with one of the cameramen and having given him my best stony stare, I was forced to whisper dire threats in his ear about the use of his hands. I think this was somewhat lost as he had some big headphones on presumably to listen to the director and probably couldn't hear me. However, a slap on his hands from Cecilia did the trick.

So all in all, it all went very well so the director told me. Looked like a complete dog's dinner if you had asked me, but then I am not used to these things. Never seen so many bits of equipment and cables in my life but at the end it was all neatly rolled up, put into carry cases and back in the three vans.

'It will be a week or two before this goes out,' the producer told us, 'there has to be a lot of editing and then they have to create a time slot so you will get a call beforehand to warn you. With that, the personnel got into a twelve-seater minivan and left followed by the two big TV equipment trucks.

One week turned into two weeks and still there was no call from the TV people, so we just waited patiently and hoped that everything would calm down. Walt was very excited as the articles in the press had certainly increased the gates and Mabel told us that the zoo was on its way to making record profits and that she had a good chance of getting the rise she deserved for all her extra hard work. Poor deluded Mabel!

Visitors had begun to be a major problem. I think I mentioned that the main purpose of the zoo was preservation and breeding and this produced a need for very large enclosures as close as possible to the animals' natural habitats with privacy areas. This caused ongoing issues with visitors and the cries of "Where is it", "Can't see it" were very common. Our live animal displays helped enormously but led to an over-exuberance at times; a series of unfortunate events and almost a disastrous finale.

Although Larry was truly in his element, he had a serious flaw probably due to him not having been fully socialised. He

171

could not stand anyone teasing or mistreating "his" animals. If he saw anyone doing something wrong, they got to know about it very quickly even though he couldn't speak.

There was an incident with one visiting yobbo who decided he wanted to give Elsie a drink and had handed her a bottle of fizzy pop of some sort which she was trying to swallow. He had not taken the top off the bottle and Elsie was getting frustrated a distressed. As he was holding the bottle out for the third or fourth time after dropping it, Larry appeared and very roughly grabbed the bottle. The youth then tried to punch Larry and he hit him with the bottle and split pouring the contents all over him. The kid was marched to the front gates still dripping and told never to come back and thankfully that was the last we heard of it.

The next incident was harder to placate and had it not been for a good-natured visitor who had filmed the incident on her camera, Larry and the zoo could have got into trouble.

Penguin feeding time had always been popular with the keeper throwing fish to the penguins in rotation to make sure they all got some. A boy of about ten was there with his parents, and despite the warning signs, decided it would be funny to throw peanuts to the penguins. Worse, they decided it would be even funnier to throw some at the keeper as well who happened to be being assisted by Larry. Larry's response was to start pelting the family with fish.

The family threatened to sue for assault and it was only by the intervention of the proffered video that roles were suddenly reversed and the family found themselves potentially on the receiving end of a counter suit with the firm evidence to back it up.

The family went away with hollow threats that they would never come again.

The final incident was a screamer. Literally. Some of the enclosures were open, in that the enclosures were sunken with a large wall and a dry moat under. This afforded an excellent view of the animals, as the centre of the enclosure was higher almost to the footpath level outside.

A young boy of probably three or four got over excited about seeing the big "pussy cats" close up wanted a closer look and his mother held him up on the perimeter wall and then sat him down on it. Unfortunately, in his excitement he wriggled, she did not have a proper hold on him and he toppled off the wall luckily landing on a bed of sand that cushioned his fall of probably about twelve feet. Now leopards are quite unpredictable and to relieve some of the boredom of their existence you could not blame them for seeing something new for them to play with suddenly drop into their home. Leopard play includes a sort of patting often with their claws out and there can be some very nasty injuries. Worse, if they get really mad, they will go for the throat then it is a one-way trip to the morgue, that is if there is anything left.

Shrieks and cries from the parents, who frankly were to blame, brought an assistant keeper running to the scene. There was a lot of unhelpful advice and a brief attempt by the father to climb the wall and rescue his son. The assistant keeper had the good sense to call for help, shout for quiet and tell the boy not to move. By now, two leopards were moving closer out of sheer curiosity. They had already been fed that day but no doubt, an extra tasty morsel might be quite tempting for them.

To this day, from what I heard, no one could tell me how he got there or where he had come from and my only guess afterwards is that he had some way of knowing that there was trouble there and had reacted accordingly.

The assistant keeper told me that while they were trying to distract the leopards and not succeeding too well, Larry appeared from inside their enclosure presumably by the back service gate and calmly walked towards them. He put his hands on the back of each of them, bent down, drew them together and started making a small sound. One of the leopards rolled on to its back while the other sat down beside Larry.

Someone had had the foresight to fetch a long ladder and Larry motioned to the assistant keeper to climb down into the enclosure. The ensuing rescue and the climb up the ladder with the child over his shoulder were met with rapturous applause.

The child was bruised but otherwise unhurt, the parents were in hysterics of relief and Larry had disappeared.

That day, Larry became a hero and the darling of the press.

Chapter 13
Disaster Strikes

Now not all the press were supportive and we still saw some periodic criticism even about the rescue itself but in the main, these were shouted down by the volume of praise and interest from the other papers. The local TV was particularly happy and wanted to do a series.

So, a star was born and Larry, unassuming as he was, began to blossom and grow in confidence. I had long given up hope of him talking and I had just reluctantly come to the conclusion that he couldn't. Not really too sad because Larry made up for it in many other ways and all in all, he was a really good kid.

He and Cecilia had formed a very special bond and they were our "A" team. Each day, sometimes twice they would put on a show which was a delight to watch. The visitors were enthralled. Cecilia, as I said, would do the commentary. She was very articulate and very easy on the eye and I think I saw quite a lot of men drifting off during her talks.

Larry during these talks would bring out favourite animals and at time, we had to temper their enthusiasm or we would have been chasing loose animals around all day long. The zoo hierarchy were in raptures and there was even talks going on about having a kind of covered arena with fixed tiered seating to accommodate the visitors. As it were, the zoo had to adopt an all ticket access to the visitor pavilion to try and control the numbers.

The daily routine for Larry looked something like this although it was apt to vary and it did. Ambling around comfortably the following afternoon, I was joined, unusually by Walt. 'Got a minute?' he said, 'Something strange.'

'Yes sure, Mr Whitlam, nice to see you out and about.'

'Have you had any strange approaches from strangers?'

'No, why do you ask?'

'This morning, I was in the meeting room dictating notes of a speech I have to give to Mabel and we both heard a noise. So, I went into her office but there was nothing untoward. Then I went into my office and there was a man there kneeling on the floor looking at something. When he saw me, he fumbled about then quickly got up and muttered something about feeling unwell and the way to the sick bay. Odd thing was, when he got up he suddenly picked up a hat that he had left on the desk and crammed it on to his head. His whole demeanour was odd and I was so surprised that I just said something inane about him seeing a doctor while he scurried out without another word.

'Later, when I sat down in my office, I found there were a number of personnel files that he had obviously tried to hide when I walked in, he simply stuffed under the desk.'

'I will keep my eyes open. So, what did he look like?'

'I would say unremarkable. Darkish hair, clean-shaven, average height. The only unusual thing I can remember is his dark suit, shirt and tie and that hat. The hat was very unusual. It wasn't a homburg or a trilby. It had a wider brim than usual, no band and a kind of crease in the front.'

'Listen, just a hunch, but there has been a lot of publicity recently about the boy, so I would not be surprised if someone is trying to find out a bit more than we are telling. Press will stoop pretty low and I wouldn't put it past them. Just in case, keep an eye on him, will you?'

'Will do.' And with that, Walt strode off and I continued with my daily duties. *Probably a good idea,* I thought, *if I give Larry a proper schedule, not so much for him, but for us so we have a better idea where he is at any time.*

This idea took root and ten minutes later, I had sketched out a programme and fixed it to his locker plus a copy which I would carry with me.

Morning seven am. Mucking out and feeding animals.

Nine o'clock breakfast with Joe, Molly and Cecilia sometimes joined by Spencer and even Marjorie. Freddy and Emily had an open invitation but preferred their own company for some reason.

Ten o'clock more mucking out and feeding animals.

Eleven o'clock until noon, visitor pavilion.

Noon lunchtime.

After this, Larry would repair to the island and play with the gibbons then have a snooze.

Three o'clock, a blast from an air horn would alert him that the second performance of the day was upon him and he needed to go and fetch an animal (or two) for the show in half an hour's time. That, his time was his own and he would normally spend this somewhere, usually in one of the animal enclosures.

There then developed a further "spin-off" which Cecilia no doubt had a hand in which we called the parade. We had done this before with Elsie the elephant and the better-natured camel but these two had taken it to new heights.

Larry would often be seen wandering hand in hand through the zoo with Blimp whom he dressed in a spare zoo uniform complete with my hat, the one that had seen better days. Visitors would be able to shake Blimp's free hand or pose with him for photos. Blimp carried a sort of open pouch cum money belt in which visitors were invited to place a donation for the photo op. Blimp at times got quite carried away with this and we had a lot of trouble getting the money off him sometimes.

This then developed further with Blimp and Raymond sitting on Blimp's shoulders. Larry and Cecilia then had plans to be a little more adventurous with different planned combinations. Blimp riding on Elsie. This would have worked, as Elsie was a docile old soul.

Next was Blimp riding on the camel. This would definitely have had problems as the camel did not like Blimp despite a good talking to from Larry and Blimp did not like the camel. Couldn't blame him, nor did I.

177

Walt put his foot down to these last two ideas which led to some pouting and bad behaviour, but they managed to sneak in another variation.

This involved Cecilia hand in hand with Blimp dressed of course in his uniform and then two female orangutans then Larry on the outside. This peculiar chain would wander up and down the main boulevard finally alighting at a picnic table much to the disgust of Molly. Big visitor attraction.

It was during one of the performance in the visitor pavilion when I happened to be free when I first spotted the man. He was not especially unusual except for a strange broad-brimmed hat and his overall shiftiness. The hat attracted attention because not many people wore them and it was undoubtedly the one and same described by Walt. It was however, his stillness and intense gaze that was really eye catching. He was staring intently at Larry, watching his every move and at the end of the session quietly slipped away and I thought nothing more about it except to warn Larry about talking to strangers and letting the others in on my concerns.

The following day, Larry joined us for lunch as usual complete with blimp still wearing his uniform which by now was beginning to develop a life of its own. He sat down on the bench with us.

Molly emerged from the servery. 'It's bad enough that we have to have the chimp's party here every weekend but I'm damned if I'm going to eat my lunch with that monkey here,' she exclaimed.

'He's not a monkey, he's an ape,' I said, 'why have you worked in a zoo all these years if you don't like animals?'

'I like animals all right but in their own places and this is not it. Besides I've had a couple of run-ins with this one.'

This was actually true. It had started one day when Larry was not paying attention and Blimp wandered into the servery and helped himself to the fruit. Not some fruit but all of it. Then chased up the adjoining tree by Molly with a broom he proceeded to throw fruit at her which she then made Larry clear up.

But worse was to come. The very regular trips out of his enclosure had given Blimp an additional confidence and this coupled with a natural mischievous nature led to a self-taught proclivity of "goosing" women.

Usually if not watched, this would take the form of a quick stroke or pinch of a women's bottom and for some reason, the recipient usually found this very amusing. Joe and I thought he must have some Italian blood in him somewhere. Sadly, it did not end there and the next trick was to sneak up behind a woman, put his long arms around her and grab her boobs. I will never understand human nature because if we had tried that we would have been in for a good slapping or possibly even a day in court and an entry on the sex offenders' register.

The main problem was the first time he tried this was on Molly who was busy at one of the service stations bending down to get us some more sugar. At first, I think she must have been Joe being playful until she saw the hairy forearms and she freaked.

Blimp, I think, thought he was being affectionate and being spurned did not sit well with him because he shot up the same tree and flatly refused to budge. In the end, we had to push Larry up the tree to talk him down.

The relationship between Blimp and Molly had been very strained since that day, and she spent a lot of time looking over her shoulder when he was around.

The following week, I was watching them again in the visitor pavilion. This time, Larry had the cobra, the one that had been de-fanged, and looking around I noticed the same man again. Actually, I noticed his hat first. This time at the end of the talk, he tried to approach Larry, said a couple of words which I could not make out and tried to take Larry by the arm. Larry's reaction was quite startling as he literally went white, pulled his arm away and ran off with the cobra.

I managed to get close enough to the man to say "please keep away from the keepers when they are holding our animals" and he gave me a startled look and sloped off. I decided not to follow when a voice said behind me, 'Be careful, Ben, there is danger here.'

'Professor,' I exclaimed, 'nice to see you again, what do you mean?'

'I think you should make sure that Larry is all right then you and I need to have a talk. There are some things that I haven't told you and you need to be aware. Can we meet somewhere quiet and bring the other three if they are available.'

'Sounds very mysterious, Professor, what is this all about?'

'I will tell you what I know or what I think I know when we are all together and Larry is safe.'

'If you come with me, Larry will be putting the cobra back in the vivarium and we can catch him there. I will call the others to meet us in the admin block in ten minutes.'

'Here is Larry,' who was emerging from the reptile house, 'Larry, will you finish now and go off to the island. Make sure you use the boat and tie it up on the far side.' Larry gave me a quizzical look but as usual did what he was told and jogged off.

Ten minutes later, the other three arrived and I introduced the Professor to Mabel and asked to use the meeting room.

'Before we start,' I said, 'I am just going to alert the security guys to this man and he shouldn't be difficult for them to spot. I will also ask them to check his entrance ticket.'

'I cannot prove anything I am about to tell you. A lot of it is based on hearsay,' said the Professor quietly, 'but all this recent publicity jogged something in my memory and an event which happened over seventy years ago when I was eight or nine years old.

'I think I told you that I was born and grew up in the village where I now live. It is a small tight-knit community but in my youth, it was even more so as there were no holiday cottages part-time residents. We knew everyone and everyone knew us.

'One of the local farmers, one day, found a little waif of a girl who he found in his barn. It turned out that she had been living there for some time, tucked away in the hayloft and living on raw free-range eggs and milk straight from the cows. Being kind people, they took the little girl in expecting to have word that eventually her parents would come looking for her. They never did, so being childless they decided that she should remain with them and for many months, she was happy with them. Her name was Lisa.

'Now comes what I think is the relevant point. Each year, the village had a fête where people brought animals and produce, played games, all the usual things.

'The story has it that during this warm, summer day, the flowers which had been put on display started to wilt. The little girl went into the tent, went down the row and the flowers sprang back into full bloom. After that, I was told, the farmers would invite her into their fields and wherever she walked, the crops would improve and become more bountiful. Mind, I am just telling you what I heard. I didn't witness it myself but I remember playing with Lisa who was about six or seven years old. She would sing to us and seemed happy to join in with all our games and activities.

'One day, so the story goes, two strangers turned up who had apparently heard somehow about the girl. They were turned away by the suspicious villagers as kids in those days were treated as communal property and alternatively protected or chastised as required by whoever was nearest.

'Soon after this, the little girl disappeared, never to be seen or heard of again. The police were advised but could do nothing as there was no record of where she had appeared from in the first place.

'I overheard the old lady talking to my parents saying "it was the Watchers that took her".

'I asked my parents what this meant after the old lady had gone back to her house and I was told that this was part of the old legend and the Watchers were people whose job it was to watch over the special ones, the Feyr, and to protect the knowledge of their special abilities from mankind and to avoid their exploitation. They said it was just a story and she would turn up but she never did.

'Now we have a situation, where Larry has been thrust into the limelight, so to speak, and suddenly a strange man appears. I have seen this man several times now; you tell me you have seen him twice. What you don't see is that there is another man with him. They are together but they make sure they stand apart so as to not attract attention.

'Maybe I had some sort of premonition about this so I have been making it my business to visit the zoo regularly. I am now sure that Larry is in danger and I believe he has felt this himself when he was approached today. You saw his re-action.'

'Yes, he was certainly frightened. I have never seen him like that before. There is one thing though, Professor, you said you have been visiting regularly but I have only ever seen you here once and I don't miss much.'

There was a long pause and then the Professor looked around cautiously and said quietly, 'I didn't say that I had come here.'

'Sorry, I don't understand.'

'Think about our conversation at the house,' he said, 'sometimes you don't have to physically be there.'

I must have looked very blank, because he sighed and then continued.

'Ben, I am going to have to trust you, but you must keep this a secret between us. I have never even talked about this to Joe and Molly. You must clear your mind first of all as you are experiencing a natural resistance to what you already know and feel. I told you about the little girl I played with in the village when I was just a boy. Well, she left something or awakened something dormant in me. I can sit in my chair, close my eyes and concentrate on a place or person and it gradually appears to me. When this happens, I am completely deaf and blind but the picture forms in my mind. It is called remote viewing. You must tell no one or even hint at it.

'There are some countries and their agencies who take this very seriously and their intentions are not strictly honourable. The Russians even have an institute dedicated to the study of these types of phenomena.'

'I have always had an open mind,' I said, 'but this is straining things a bit.'

'It's perfectly true, Ben, you have the proof already. It is in you now and all you have to do is allow this and not block it out.'

'Listen to the Professor, Ben, Joe and I have also had this same feeling of danger and it is getting stronger. I suggest we formulate some sort of plan to protect him as best we can. You know how naïve he is. An innocent in many ways so he needs watching,' said Molly.

'Is there any way you can prevail on him to stay indoors at night,' said Cecilia, 'at least there are loads of people around during the day.'

'Tried that before and he just climbs out of the window to be with his precious gibbons,' said Joe, 'Molly was getting worried about him now winter is approaching being out there on the island all night.'

'Larry will be warned already about this man, so we don't need to alarm him further. I think he will be OK as long as he stays in the zoo and has people around him,' said the Professor.

Word went out to all the staff to keep a look out for any people acting strangely or approaching Larry. The problem was with his new celebrity status that many people wanted to take photos with, him ask for an autograph or simply just to speak to him.

Finally, the day came when our worst fears were realised.

'Have you seen Larry?' said Cecilia, 'we were meant to be doing a lecture together in the pavilion but he didn't show.'

'I last saw him heading for the island so I will go and check,' I replied, 'probably having a doze.'

When I got to the island, I noticed that the boat was still moored up. This was strange as we had told Larry off several times for wading across, sometimes with his boots on, and at last, he had begun to listen. I clambered into the little boat with an ever-increasing sinking feeling in my stomach which was fully realised after I had checked out the gibbon sanctuary fully.

In a slight panic, I called the others and asked them to start checking while I rowed back.

I got back to the shore, tied up the boat to be met by Joe. 'Bad news, I just checked with the main gate and Larry was seen about an hour ago.'

'Let's go and talk to them, Joe.'

Joe and I ran off to the main gate to talk to the receptionist. 'It wasn't me who saw him, it was Janet in the shop. I was busy.'

'Janet, can we have a word please. What did you see?'

'Larry was in here, looking at the fluffy toy animals and helping me to arrange them when a man came in and started talking to him,' said Janet, 'didn't think anything of it at the time because everyone wants to talk to him. Next minute, I saw him walking out the front door and I heard the man say he had an injured animal in the car and needed help with it.'

'What did this man look like?'

'About forty-ish, light-brown hair, overcoat, ordinary,' she said.

'Did he have a hat?'

'No, his hands free, but he did have gloves on which now I think about it, was a bit strange at this time of the year.'

'Then what?'

'There was an old, green van, one of those Commer things with a sliding side door. The door opened, Larry looked in to where the man was pointing, then I got distracted. When I looked back, they were all gone.'

'You didn't get the van number by any chance, Janet,' said Joe.

''Fraid not,' she replied.

'Let's go and notify the police, it can't be that hard to find an old, green van. Better go tell the others.'

We met at the picnic table with Molly, Cecilia and me. 'He's been snatched,' I said, 'somehow he must have been enticed by the story of the injured animal and maybe it all happened too quickly before he sensed the danger.'

'I am going out to look for him in the car,' said Joe.

'I'll take mine as well,' said Cecilia.

The three of us set off leaving Molly distraught behind us supposedly awaiting news. Secretly, we knew that there would be none. He was lost.

Hours and hours of driving, repeatedly calling the police but no sign, no news. Spencer and Marjorie joined in the search. We were helpless and so it continued for weeks and weeks.

'We need a plan to cover this,' said Joe, 'or we are going to get every Tom Dick and Harry asking questions about why he's not here anymore.'

'How about we say that the zoo has sent him to look at some new animals to see if they are suitable for their zoo,' said Cecilia.

'Perfect,' I said, 'maybe we should suggest to Walt to make a press statement before the questions start. Take the initiative.'

'I'll go and see him now,' replied Joe.

'He's gone,' Molly wailed, 'they've taken him.'

Chapter 14
The Awakening

The following days and weeks were spent in turmoil. We took it in turns to excuse ourselves from work and roam the surrounding areas in a hopeless search, each day returning and comparing notes, fielding unwelcome questions from the Press and generally wandering around feeling totally useless. There was no sign; the police were coming up blank and we were losing hope.

Weeks had by now gone by and for some sort of comfort I had taken to sitting on Gibbon Island on a daily basis going over and over all the events of the previous months in the hope that something would occur.

I recalled the conversations with the Professor, in themselves strange and I remembered his tale of the little girl and the "gift" she had either given or awakened in him. I called him.

'Professor, can I talk to you about the thing you told me about in private. I have an idea,' I said.

'Hello, Ben, you sound excited, good news?'

'No, sorry, absolutely nothing. Can we talk?'

'Not over the phone if it is about "you know what",' he replied.

'Can I come and see you urgently and bring the others?'

'If you mean by the others, just the four of you, then yes.'

Six o'clock, the four of us met at our table as usual and I told them about my idea. They were sceptical, to put it mildly.

'As I said, it is just an idea. You remember that the Professor told us that acquired a special ability after he met the little girl. Well, what he did not elaborate on was that over the years, he has been very quietly honing this ability for remote viewing. Now, we four know that some of us have a sort of increased awareness or empathy after being in contact with Larry. Let us say that the Professor also has this and maybe he could use his ability to "tune-in" to Larry and give us some clue where he might be.'

'Bit far-fetched,' said Cecilia, 'why do you think this might work?'

'I don't, but let's face it, we and the police have tried everything else and it's now been several weeks and we are desperate.'

'I think it's a good idea,' said Molly, 'shouldn't underestimate these things, it can't do any harm. What else did he say?'

'He wouldn't talk on the phone. We did make a promise about keeping his secret, you may recall.'

'Okay,' said Joe, 'let's go and see him tomorrow after we finish.'

The following workday dragged. A feeling of elation and hope then depression with reality re-struck. At last, we finished our evening meal or at least, the amount we were able to eat and set out for the Professor's home.

The Professor was pretending to work in his garden as we arrived though we had no doubts he was actually waiting to greet is and hear my idea. So, without further ado, we went into his cottage, sat down at his request and got on with it.

'Just come out with it, Ben,' said the Professor, not being able to hold back.

'Professor, you will recall that you told us about your special ability. When you were with Larry, did you feel anything different about him or in yourself like a tingling or warmth flowing through your arms?'

'At my age, hot flushes, tingling, aches and pains are daily occurrences so it's hard to tell.'

'Let me try something else on you,' I said, feeling a bit down hearted by his response.

'Can you pick up people with your ability?'

'Yes, sometimes, but not always the ones I want to,' he replied, 'but I think I see what you might be getting at. You think I may have obtained some sort of mental link or impression from Larry and I might be able to us this to "home-in" on his frequency to try and find where he is.'

'It's a long shot, I know, but we have tried everything else.'

'I have never tried anything like this, but I am prepared to give it a go.'

'Should we wait here?' Molly said.

'No, I need complete quiet to be able to focus and when I do, my sight and hearing will disappear as I told you. Just leave me to it.'

We took our leave and set off back homewards. I was not sure what we should have expected and maybe we had raised our hopes too high, so it was a nice surprise three days later when the Professor telephoned.

'Can you come here this weekend? Not just for the day but be prepared to stay Saturday and Sunday. Don't ask, can't speak over the phone.'

'We will be there first thing tomorrow,' I promised on behalf of us all knowing that they would readily agree.

The following morning, we were at the cottage by nine o'clock, anxious to find out whether my idea had had any merit. The Professor looked very tired and drawn with puffiness around his eyes and even more prominent cheekbones than usual. To our joint annoyance and being centre stage, the Professor had decided to "milk" this one. So, we waited.

'I have news,' he suddenly burst out, 'Larry is alive. You were right, I can feel or more accurately sense him. The sense is very weak and it has taken a lot of time and concentration to even come up with this small piece of information. So, we need to take this further. I have asked you all to come here for the weekend for two reasons.

'The first, you know. This has to be kept top secret between the five of us. If this got out, the rest of my life would be a living hell. The second reason is going to take a lot of trust on your parts as I cannot really explain it, but I think you will quickly understand my thoughts.

'Let me start on the premise that we all have a special place in our thoughts for the boy. These thoughts go beyond a

188

normal care and love for a child to a higher level of empathy. Have you never found it strange that Larry almost anticipates what we are going to say or what you want him to do? I would put to you that we share some sort of mental linkage.

'Let us run with this idea and think about whether we would have a greater chance or better and clearer contact if we were linked together in some way.

'I have exhausted myself over the last few days and try as I might, I can get no nearer to him so I need your help. What do you say?'

'Just tell us what you want us to do,' said Joe, 'we have come this far so everything possible or even impossible is worth trying.'

'We are going to have a séance,' explained the Professor, 'but not just any old ordinary séance. We are going to try and mentally link then help me project. I have found that when I get tired, my ability weakens, so you are all going to be my mental or psychic battery.

'For the rest of the morning, you should each find your own private place and think of the child and try to connect. No real instruction booklet on this one but it might help if you try and clear your minds as best you can. I am going off for a lie down, as I haven't really slept for the last three days and I need to be at my best.'

The Professor left us in the living room and we heard him making his way up the creaky old staircase to, presumably, his bedroom.

'Molly and I are going to go for a walk,' said Joe, 'find somewhere nice and peaceful and do as he suggests.'

'We'll come too,' said Cecilia.

'No, you won't,' replied Molly, 'you go find your own place with Ben.'

Thank you and good idea, I thought. Molly looked at me and slowly shook her head as if knowing what I was thinking. Spoilsport!

There is something about the English countryside, that imbues a feeling of peace and calm, that is unless it is pouring with rain and blowing a gale. However, that day was what we call balmy and going down the lane; over a stile and across a newly harvested field, we found our own little copse where we settled down on a blanket we had carried with us. No sign of Joe and Molly or anybody else for that matter.

'I know what you are thinking, Mr Ben,' said Cecilia.

'I haven't even started focusing yet, Cecilia.'

'I don't have to start focusing,' she replied, 'it's written all over your face.'

'What is?' I asked innocently.

'I would call it unregulated lust.' *This girl knows me too well.*

'Can't help it. Beautiful girl, romantic place, deep feelings for you. Is it that bad?'

'Time and a place, Ben, time and a place.'

There's a one-liner there, I thought, *but best not to break the mood, at least what mood there was, which was very quickly disappearing.*

'What did you think of all that?' she said.

'To be honest, Cecilia, there have been so many things these last few months that I don't think that anything would surprise me anymore.'

'So where do we fit in, Ben?'

'I think we fit very well.'

'You're going to make this conversation difficult, aren't you?'

'Sorry, natural defence system was cutting in there for a moment.'

'Why do you need one with me?'

'Habit.'

'Be serious.'

I'm not going to get away alive at this rate, I thought, *so...*

'The truth is, Cecilia, is that I am terrified by the intensity of my own feelings for you, so I kind of leave the door open just in case.'

'In case of what?' She started a slow smile and I was not sure what I should say next, so I went quiet for a time and then said, 'In case you stop loving me, I suppose.'

Cecilia got up and started walking around the tree clearly exasperated. 'You really are a bit thick sometimes, Ben, you have all these blockers and it is really annoying. You're not a stupid man, so you need to get some home truths into your thick head.'

This wasn't the way I thought the rest of the morning would be going and my lusty thoughts were not only being dashed on the rocks but swept away with the ebb tide.

She came and sat down and took my hand. *Best not to say anything,* I thought, *it's going to be wrong.* I knew this for sure.

'How long have we known each other? No. don't say anything, I need to explain this very carefully. When we first met, I was not in the market for a serious relationship but something happened. It wasn't just you, it was a feeling that sparked between us. I felt a calming, an inner glow and a feeling that we had been brought together. It was as if Larry had acted like a catalyst to bring our feelings out for each other. That is the only way to describe it.

'As far as losing me or me stopping loving you, you can get those ideas right out of your head. How's that?'

'I'm going to have to stop you talking somehow.'

'What had you got it mind?'

'I'll show you.'

Two hours later, we heard a bell ringing in the distance and we reluctantly detached ourselves to try to figure out what the noise was. It turned out to be the Professor who had one of those old school hand bells and was calling us back like a pair of naughty school kids. Funnily enough, I actually felt like one. We arrived at the cottage at almost exactly the same time of Joe and Molly.

As we went through the garden gate, Molly gently took a small twig out of Cecilia's hair and gave me a knowing look but kept quiet.

'I have set up the dining table,' said the Professor.

We were ushered into the dining room and in the centre was one of those old round oak tables with a highly polished inlaid top and a single spreading pedestal support with ornate carvings. We sat down to allotted positions, me holding Cecilia's hand on one side and Joe's on the other.

'How have we got on this morning?' asked the Professor, 'Have you had some good clear thoughts?'

Molly looked at me and I must have blushed because Cecilia's hand tightened on mine and she stifled a smile.

'I think we should close our eyes and just try to clear our minds. Think of something that is calming like clouds or a stream or corn swaying in the wind. You get the idea. Now if this works, you will find that I will not be able to see or hear you. I don't even know what happens or even whether I can speak. It is very draining so please do not interrupt or break the circle. If you need a comfort break, have it now.'

We declared ourselves happy and proceeded with our instructions. Every now and then, I would peek out to see if anything was happening. The minutes just ticked away and I could swear that the clock was getting louder but this was probably just an illusion, as other senses seemed to fade away. At one point, I thought I had dozed off as images and memories of Larry came and went.

Perhaps I did doze off because it seemed like I had been sitting there for a long time so I broke the rules and opened my eyes. To my complete surprise, the other four had theirs open and were looking at me.

'Welcome back,' said the Professor, 'I wish we could have taped your expressions to see.'

'Anything happened. What was I doing?'

'You were talking to Larry,' said Molly, 'you seemed to be giving him his work schedule. Talking your head off for the last ten minutes.'

'Sorry.'

No reason, but part of this experiment worked. I got a much clearer picture of Larry. I can tell you that he is not frightened but he is very unhappy about being away from the zoo and you all. He is being held somewhere. I can see a room where he is. It has a high ceiling and it is a bit dilapidated. There is a single window but it looks like it is shuttered and barred. There is a bed, a wooden kitchen chair and a single sideboard. Apart from that, there is nothing on the walls that I can see. He is there on his own looking at an animal encyclo-paedia and there is a food tray on the floor.

The positive thing is that he knows that I am looking through him and I feel that he is taking some comfort from that. Now, I am too tired to continue so it's time to eat and then I suggest we relax and get an early night then try again tomorrow.

'How about I cook us all something?' said Molly.

'Splendid idea,' replied the Professor, 'with my cooking skills, you may not make it to the morning.'

Molly did us proud with a rather limited choice of food-stuffs in the larder and we found ourselves beyond tired with all the anxiety and mental exhaustion so it was later than we had hoped the following morning when we reassembled in the dining room.

'We need to try this again,' said the Professor, 'but with a bit more focus and concentration. So please clear your minds everyone.'

The clock ticked louder and louder again; I dared to peek to see what the others were doing but they, unlike me, seemed to be behaving themselves. Every now and then, Cecilia would give my hand a squeeze, for, I suppose, some mutual reassurance. It must have been some two hours later when the clock chimed eleven o'clock and the Professor exclaimed, 'Now that's better, my link was much stronger. I have no idea why. Maybe you are improving or maybe the good night's sleep did the trick. Anyway, I got back into the room where the boy is but this time, the shutters were open so I could see through the window. As I thought, the building is quite formal with high ceilings and low windows so that would put it in probably the Victorian or Edwardian eras. Outside, there is no sign of paths or lawns. The surrounding area is heavily wooded on rising ground so the house must stand in a valley somewhere. The problem is I don't know where. There is one very strange thing though. Here we are at the end of Novem-ber when the trees should have shed their leaves and plants died back ready for winter, yet the area of garden I could see was in full bloom. It could be that the woodland protects the property and there is some sort of microclimate there. Very odd though.'

'So what do we do next if we can't locate the place?' asked Joe.

'I have an idea on that and it involves Molly,' answered the Professor. 'We know that Molly has, let's call them abilities, particularly I know that she has the ability to dowse.'

'I had forgotten about that,' said Molly, 'I used to wander around with my uncle as a girl on his farm with a hazel twig to pick up underground streams or springs. He was always very pleased and said I should make a living doing it. It's been a long time though.'

'It seems to me that what we are trying to achieve is an awakening of senses that some or all of us have in varying degrees then attempting to amplify them as we have before. Now, the next stage is going to be even more difficult as it relies on Molly being able to take her ability to a higher level. This is what we do.

'Molly, you may or may not be aware that dowsing need not be restricted to finding water. I think we spoke about this not that long ago. Dowsers can find minerals, objects and even in some cases people. You have no doubt seen and heard about psychics helping the police in murder or missing person's case. Is this not a form of dowsing and in some cases coupled with remote viewing?

'I want you to concentrate on the boy and the description of the property. I have an idea that he is somewhere on or near the moor as everything seems to stem from this area. I am going to fetch a map and a variety of devices. Just as in dowsing in the fields, some people work better with different objects like copper rods or a pendulum.'

The Professor got up and went to the cupboard in the corner and produced a rolled up map and some instruments. There was a plumb bob, a compass and a brass pointer which looked like the minute hand off a large clock. He unrolled the map and smoothed it flat on top of the dining table. 'Now please sit in the same places as before,' he said, 'hold hands like before except this time Joe and I will put one hand each on Molly's shoulders as she will need her hands free. I have no idea whether this will work but I have run out of any other ideas.'

We assembled around the table as the Professor had instructed and closed our eyes. I once again set my mind back to the wonderful times we had had with Larry and the delight he had brought to our lives. The clock ticked on and on and had it not been for that, I would have thought that time itself was standing still. I was beginning to get a headache no doubt with all the brainpower being expended when I heard a small noise.

'Something is coming through,' said Molly quietly, 'can someone pass me a pencil or crayon please.'

We opened our eyes and Joe took the pencil out of his top pocket which he always carried. 'Here you are, Molly,' he said.

'Can you pass me that pointy arrow thing?' asked Molly. 'Good. Now I am going to balance it on the paper and see what happens.' Nothing did.

'I need to be in contact with it,' she said, 'what can we use?'

'How about we turn one of those little saucers upside down; you hold it and then put the pointer on top,' said Cecilia, 'that might work.'

'Good idea, Cecilia, brains and beauty.'

It took a bit of time to get the arrangement balanced and we reverted back to our positions except this time, with our eyes wide open.

'There, it moved,' exclaimed Cecilia suddenly, 'I'm sure I wasn't imagining it. Yes, there it goes again, it's swinging around.'

The pointer slowly revolved clockwise, then settled in a new position and stopped.

'Has someone got a ruler or something with a straight edge?' asked Molly. 'Thanks, that'll do,' as I handed her an eighteen inch piece of wood that was used to hold the window sash open. 'Now, I am going to draw a line across this map where the arrow thing is pointing. There. Now I think we should start again; I will move the pointer into a different place on the map and see what happens.'

This time, the result was almost immediate and the pointer swung around in a different direction, trembled and stopped. 'Now we draw another line in that direction,' she said.' There. Now my guess is where the two intersect is the place we are looking for. "X" marks the spot – I hope!'

'Professor, do you know this place?' I asked.

'I know the area but not that place specifically. Let me get the Ordnance Survey sheet out, as it will be a larger scale with more detail.'

The OS sheet was old and somewhat frayed but serviceable, and we quickly identified the area that the larger map had indicated.

'I was right,' said the Professor, 'here is the wooded valley, you can tell by the contours and there is a structure there in the middle of the wood, but I can't see any road or path going to it.'

'We need to go and scout it out,' I said.

'Yes,' said Cecilia, 'let's go now.'

'You're not coming.'

'Who says?'

'I say, we are dealing here with at least two kidnappers and they may get desperate. They could harm you, harm Larry, goodness knows what so you will have to trust me. We three will go and you two ladies can hold the fort here.'

'Can I point out very gently,' replied Cecilia, 'that to put it politely the Professor is somewhat advanced in years and in a struggle about as much use as a chocolate teapot. Sorry, Professor.'

'It's all right, my dear, no offence taken. You are of course right but I need to be there. Joe and Ben will look after me but they could not look after you and Molly at the same time, so I concur with Ben.'

'They're ganging up on us, Molly,' complained Cecilia.

'We'll give them this one, just this once, my luvver,' replied Molly.

Chapter 15
The House on the Moor

Thinking back on it, it was probably not the best time to go rooting around on the moor. Many had gone astray, never to be found again, but the weather was dry and we were enthused and at the same time apprehensive about the task ahead. It turned out that the area we needed to get to was on the edge of the moor some four miles away and the route need not follow the most direct route but could skirt around the edge of the more barren areas. We arrived there in less than thirty minutes and after going up and down the road a few times decided to park up in a layby to plan the next move.

We were sitting in the car when we noticed a woman walking down the path which ran obliquely from the higher ground towards the road. She was tall with grey hair tied back in a bun and carrying a wicker basket on her hip. She was probably in her late sixties and had on a long calf-length brown skirt; green-checked blouse and a knitted woollen shawl. As she approached the intersection of the path and road, she suddenly stopped, stiffened and looked directly at the three of us in the car. I noticed she had a pair of knitted gloves on her hands but her forearms were bare which seemed unusual.

The reaction from the Professor in the passenger seat was even stranger. 'Wait here,' he said, 'I won't be long.' With that, he opened the door and eased himself out of the car, reached in and grabbed his walking stick and started up the hill. She in turn, started down the hill and they met together a few feet in front of our car.

'Hello Lisa, it's been a long, long time,' he said.

'Bob Lofthouse, indeed it has. I knew that someday, someone would find me and here you are. It's been a long wait and I actually started to believe it would never happen. You've come for the boy.'

'Yes, Lisa, we have.'

'It's not what you think, you know, his place is with us.'

'Then why is he unhappy and locked in a room?'

'How did you know that?'

'I think you already know the answer to that one.'

'Curious, we had now got out of the car. Ben, Joe, this is Lisa. We knew each other when we were children.'

'I know who these two are,' said Lisa, 'you both work at the zoo.'

'We need to take Larry with us,' I said.

'Who is Larry? Is that what you call the boy? That's not his name.'

'We need to talk, Lisa, we are not going away, there is too much at stake for the lad, you and us,' said the Professor gently.

'This is very difficult, and I don't know how the others will react. You must give me time to prepare them. Come back tomorrow and I will meet you here.'

'Sorry,' replied Joe, 'it has taken us a lot of effort to track him this far. We are not going to take the risk of having him whisked away again so it is now or it is the police.'

'I see how it is,' said the woman, 'give me an hour and I will come back and fetch you.'

'How do we get in, we haven't seen a road or path?'

'They are there but hard to find unless you know where to look.' With that, she started off down the road and suddenly disappeared through the shrubbery.

'Ben, we need to find the entrance quickly just in case they try something stupid so Professor, you stay here and we will go off in different directions to find the access. Then we will move the car up or down to it to block their escape route.'

Joe went up the hill and I went down, both of us peering through the undergrowth to try and find the entrance. Five minutes later, I heard Joe whistle and I retraced my steps back to the layby. 'It's about two hundred yards up the road and quite cleverly screened from the road,' said Joe, 'I went past it for some distance to make sure it is the only one. Did you find anything?'

'No, the banking gets steeper and steeper as you go down the hill, so it would not be possible to drive a vehicle in through the woods.'

'Well, that must be it then, we know they have a green van, so let's drive the car up there now.'

The next forty-five minutes or so seemed like an eternity when suddenly, the woman appeared from the down the hill no doubt expecting to find us still in the layby.

'You found it then, I will open the gate. You drive straight down and you will. Come to the house. I will walk down through the woods. They may not think it right us arriving together. They are not happy about you being here so be very careful what you say.'

'How many are there?' I asked.

'There are five of us altogether.'

The approach down the hill was very slow. At times, the car bottomed out on the ridge in the middle of the dirt drive. In bad weather, it would not have been accessible. My next jolt, having just banged my head on the roof with one, was the final line of trees we were approaching. Just as the Professor had said, they were in full leaf but the sight once through them was even more spectacular. There in the middle of a grove was a rather sad-looking two-storey stoner built house completely surrounded by the most wonderful array of colour.

'When I saw the garden, I was anticipating something like this,' said the Professor.

'Explain please,' said Joe, completely bemused.

'I told you about the little girl I played with who disappeared. Her name was Lisa. You just met her. When I saw the flowers in bloom, I knew there was something strange even with the explanation of the protected valley. Then, I saw her walking down the hill and I knew for sure. Do you know why she wears gloves? Well, I will tell you if you have not guessed. You remember I told you the story about the farmers' fields.

She has an ability, an ability that the world would not understand. She is kind of human nurturer or fertiliser if you want to put it more simply. She can touch the soil or plants or crops and they spring into life. She obviously wears gloves so she does not attract attention to places outside her immediate domain. I knew all along that she wasn't dead. I can't explain it. It's a sense or feeling and it was true.'

'Do you think she was kidnapped as well all those years ago?' I said.

'I am beginning to have a theory,' replied the professor, 'but let's see what they have to say for themselves.'

The woman was already waiting for us in front of the house when we arrived. We had been mistaken about the lack of driveway or paths. They were there, all right, just covered with plant growth, lichen and algae like a green carpet interspersed with wild flowers and weeds.

The house itself was bigger than I expected and was in fact three-storeys as it had rooms and windows in the roof no doubt for more affluent past times when these were occupied by servants.

'Come in, they're waiting,' said the woman.

We were ushered through as dismal hallway containing an equally dismal staircase to a room at the back of the house which in former days most probably served as a formal dining room. The house was not damp, just gloomy except for a variety of vases, ewers and even old chamber pots filled with colourful flowers.

The three of us entered the room and seated at the table were three people. The first I instantly recognised as the man with the hat at the zoo. He was middle-aged and dressed sombrely like the other three.

The next man to him was much older and had a very close resemblance, so I concluded that they were probably father and son. Correctly, as it turned out. The third person seated was a lady in almost exactly the same garb as the woman Lisa. She was much younger, again middle aged but with strands of grey hair at her temples.

We were fixed with a hostile stare. Clearly unwelcome. The older man gestured to us to sit down and began. 'We are not used to strangers here. We live a quiet life without too much to do with them outside. Lisa says you have come for the boy. Go away, he does not belong to you. He is staying with us, his own kind.'

Well, I thought, *that has set the scene.*

'Thank you for inviting us into your home,' said the Professor, 'I think it would be a good idea if we introduced ourselves first and then you can tell us a bit about yourselves.'

'We know who you are, all right, my son and I have been watching you at the zoo,' said the older man gruffly, 'you don't have a clue what you are doing.'

'I think you know we do,' replied the Professor, 'and what we don't know, then we have a very good idea so let us not play games with each other. I know there is a lot at stake here and you guard your privacy here for a good reason.'

The older man turned his chair slightly without getting up and half turned away. 'Tell them the whole story,' said Lisa, 'they must know a lot otherwise they would never have found us. Somehow, they know about the boy as well.'

The older man thought about it for some time, sighed and then rose from the chair. 'My name is Jeremiah and this is our son, Jacob. The women here are Lisa, my wife and Jacob's wife, Sarah. The only other person living here is Edward who we call Eddy and you call Larry.

'Yes, Lisa is the little girl that you knew as a child and she does indeed have abilities. Those special abilities were becoming more and more obvious so my father, long since passed away, took the decision to rescue her from prying eyes and those that would have one day have taken advantage. My father brought her here to safety and we have protected her ever since. Many years ago, she consented to be my wife and we have lived here peacefully until this day.'

'So where did Lisa come from?' asked Joe.

Lisa was the product of a liaison between a local farmer's son and an orphaned girl who worked on their farm. The lad's parents did not approve of the match so the couple would meet in secret. It is a story as old as humanity itself and sooner or later, the girl became pregnant and was forced off the farm to live in a cave on the edge of the moor. The son would bring her food but in those conditions, the poor girl did not have a chance and died shortly after giving birth. The son brought the baby home and confessed to his parents who allowed him to keep the child at the farm. However, the parents were cruel to the kid and forced her to live in the barn. After much torment, the little girl ran away and ended up found in a barn in your village. The son was coerced by his parents not to try find her.

'What is this got to do with you?' I asked.

'Good question, Ben, isn't it? Our family goes back before history was even recorded. We are part of this place and it has been our family's sacred duty to watch over and protect any special people we hear about or find. Some evade our help and manage to live out their lives with their abilities hidden. Some are more forthright but have abilities which may not have any interest to outsiders.

'Some people call us the Watchers. As good a name as any. The duty is passed down through the male line generation by generation. My son, Jacob, here is the last as he and his wife are barren.'

'Where does Larry, I mean Eddy fit in to all this?'

'The boy is special. You know that and unfortunately, thanks to you, so do a lot of other people. They will hound him, exhibit him, examine him like a lab rat and make his life hell. Then when they have finished with him, they will go looking for others like him. That is why we had to protect him and we acted the way we did because you would not have understood.'

'Where did Eddy come from?'

'Similar story to Lisa. Eddy was born on a farm of doting parents. The father was very much in love with his mother but she also died in childbirth. You must remember that in those days, this was quite common especially in remote and rural areas where medical help was scarce. The father lost his reason and started to blame the child for his wife's death. Irrational, I know but it happens and eventually, the child spent more and more time roaming the moor and communing with the wild ponies until he was almost feral himself. Then, we understand, after a particularly bad beating, he simply ran away and fetched up at your zoo no doubt lured by the animals he loves.'

'So, in both these cases, nobody came looking for them,' I said, 'don't you find that strange?'

'Not really,' replied the Professor, 'these are remote rural communities where people get up before daybreak and go to bed after dark. There is not time to socialise and for many an annual trip to the fair is all the interaction they get. Child mortality was very common and people buried their own often without any reference to the authorities or church.'

'So back to Eddy, what do you propose to do with him?' I said.

'We will keep him safe and protect him and his special abilities from the outside world and in time, he will become the new Watcher to take over one day from my son, Jacob. He will be well cared for.'

'Jeremiah,' said Lisa, 'he is not happy here. He will not eat. He is wasting away. He needs to be with his animals. That is his purpose and we are denying him that and it's killing him.'

'He has a higher purpose. I will get him some animals if it makes you feel better,' replied Jeremiah.

'Jeremiah,' she cried, 'can't you see what you are doing, I was different but he has shown that with care, he can live in the outside world. You are not a cruel man but you and Jacob cannot keep beating him for not doing what he's told. I can't stand it anymore.'

'I can see both sides of this,' said Joe, 'but should you not let the boy have a say in this. It's his life.'

'You might think I am being selfish but we have a duty to others like him and he will be the one to uphold our tradition. Now, he is too young to decide for himself,' said Jacob.

'When he is old enough, it will be too late for him to decide and you want to deny him that choice,' I said.

'I have not said anything up to now,' said Sarah, 'but you have to listen to these people. All I see at the moment is a little boy all skin and bone, bruised, scared and helpless. Maybe it is time to give up the old ways and for the special ones to deal with their own abilities. Maybe, even, it is time for the world to know.' She sat down exhausted and started weeping.

'I have made up my mind,' shouted Jeremiah, 'it is not for you to have a say in this. We have a sacred duty.'

'I have heard enough,' said Joe sternly, 'at the rate you are going, Eddy is not going to survive to be a Watcher, as you call it. Here is our position.'

He stood up.

'We are not happy about your treatment of this child. It may surprise you, though it shouldn't that we, between us have abilities, as you call them, and have direct contact with the boy so we are fully aware of his condition and what he is feeling.

'If you persist, we are going to call Ms Marjorie Hoare who is head of the social services Department in our town. She is very well aware of his case and the major factor in the fostering agreement that she has de/vised. She is not a person to trifle with. My second telephone call will be to the police who will, without doubt, wish to interview you and charge you with kidnapping. Remember also, that we have witnesses to the actual abduction and details of your green van.

'Then, after all this, your cover and privacy will be blown sky high and once, or if, you are released you will spend the rest of your lives running and hiding from the very people you wish to protect him from. In the process, we will also be exposed but we are willing to take that chance for his sake.'

Wow, Joe, I thought, *glad you are on my side.*

'My colleagues and I are now going outside for twenty minutes to let you consider what I have said. After that, you will give us your decision. I hope for your sakes and for Eddy, it will be the right one.'

The Professor and I got off our chairs and followed Joe out of the room, down the hall and out the front door. We could hear a lot of shouting and bellowing behind us.

'Did you see any guns around?' I joked.

'Not funny Ben, I know you are only trying to relieve the tension but the next twenty minutes is crucial and it really rests on how much authority that the old man has over the others and whether he thinks we are bluffing. I think even Jacob has grave concerns about this and if he is able to stand up to his father that should clinch it. If it goes the wrong way, we have to make good our threats. You might like to check that you have a signal on your phone just in case. Liable to be lots of dead areas around here especially in a valley like this.'

'It's OK,' I said, looking at my phone, 'I have two bars up.'

'This waiting bit is taking years off me,' said Joe.

'Well just think what our ladies are going through, I was nearly going to check the boot of the car to see if they had stowed away. You know we're going to pay dearly for leaving them behind, don't you?'

'They can't do much to me,' laughed the Professor.

'Surprised you have lived this long, Professor, if you believe that. Just because they are with us doesn't mean you won't be in the firing line. It's called collateral damage.'

'What did I do?'

'You agreed with us, Professor, that will be enough for them.'

'Are the twenty minutes up yet?' said Joe.

'It's been more than that, more like half an hour.'

'Give them five more minutes, then it's "hardball" time,' replied Joe.

It was more like ten minutes later when we heard a sound and the two men emerged. Jeremiah looking like thunder and Jacob expressionless. Behind them came Lisa and Sarah with Larry between them. Both women had been crying and Lisa was trying to hide a fresh mark on her face with her shawl created, no doubt, by the hand of her husband.

Larry's eyes found us and he literally jumped for joy and ran into Joe's arms then mine. After a few minutes, he relaxed and we turned him to face the other four.

'Larry, or Eddy,' said the Professor, 'you have a choice and one you must think about very hard. You can stay here and these people will promise to treat you well. They have said that they will bring you animals of your own to look after. They will not lock you in and within reason, you will have the freedom to roam around as you did once before. The alternative is that you can come back to the zoo with us. You will not always be able to do whatever you want and they will have to take your schooling more seriously than they have before. You will have a home with Molly and Joe as before and they will love and care for you as though you were their own son.

'What do you say? I know you can nod as you usually do.' He did and very vigorously.

Now it is our time to be magnanimous. I will say this to the four of you. You are welcome to visit the boy at the zoo and on occasions, we will bring him here to stay with you. When he is older, he can decide for himself whether he wants to return to you or not. That is our offer and here is my hand on it.'

Jeremiah stroked his chin, stepped forward, spat on his hand and took the Professor's hand followed by Jacob who copied him. Both women smiled and nodded and each gave Larry a hug.

'Off we go then,' said the Professor, 'I think the ladies are waiting for you.'

I drove on the way back with the Professor in the passenger seat and Joe with Larry in the back. 'By the way, Larry, should we call you Larry or Eddy?'

In response, Larry cupped his hands to his mouth and exactly copied the hooting noise of the Lar gibbon.

'I think that's your answer, Ben.'

'New life, new name, good start,' I said.

The return to the village thirty minutes later was a pantomime in itself. Cecilia had not been able to wait and had crept some hundred yards up the lane in anticipation. Molly meanwhile was gardening on the premise of keeping busy and had dug up and replanted the same rose bush three times. It wasn't even her garden!

The car stopped once we saw Cecilia who was lurking behind a bush by the side of the road no doubt surprised on how far she had wandered up the road. Molly cleared the front garden wall by a good twelve inches having completely forgotten about the half-planted rose bush.

'Time for a very late tea,' said the Professor, 'or are we too excited to eat?'

'Let's get Larry something while you tell us everything that happened and woe betides you if you miss anything out, my luvvers,' said Molly.

'We're back,' I said.

'There's still time to escape if we're quick,' whispered Joe.

'We heard that.'

'Ears like elephant's, Joe.'

'We heard that too.'

'Did you bring the white flag with you, Joe?'

'Never go anywhere without it, Ben.'

Chapter 16
A Child of God

It was now middle December and the weather had closed in. Zoo visitors were fewer and fewer and some of the animals began to appreciate what little attention they got rather than hiding away from the usual noisy throng. Joe and Molly had been doing their best to encourage Larry to sleep in his bedroom but he insisted on returning to the island each night.

'I wish we could get some sense into him,' said Molly, 'he's so thin and I don't like that chesty cough at all.'

It was quite clear that his enforced incarceration had taken its toll and it wasn't going to take some real care and bottlefuls of vitamins to get him back to full strength.

For our part, all Joe and I could do was make sure the main hut was as comfortable and weatherproof as we could so we spent some time filling holes in the walls, floor and roof. I, in turn, tried to concentrate on giving Larry more and more inside jobs.

One morning, the phone was ringing as I got out of the shower. It was Joe who was always an early riser. 'Can you come down here right away? There is something very strange going on. Tell you when you get here.'

I got dressed and on my motorbike and was there within twenty minutes. Joe was waiting for me at the main gate.

'I was called out about five this morning by the police whom said they had complaints from a lot of our neighbours about the noises from the zoo.' *This was strange*, I thought, as we are pretty well insulated here by the hill and woods at the back and across the road is just the supermarket and the school. But sure enough, when I arrived, there was a devil of a noise going on. Roaring, hooting, rasping, shrieking, every noise that every creature could make. No wonder the police had complaints. They had asked me to meet the policeman at the main gate. I could hardly hear what the policeman was saying. So, I was just trying to think what to say to him, to placate him and allow me to go and check when suddenly the noise stopped. Then, not one sound.

With that, the policeman left probably thinking I was some sort of wizard and I went into the zoo proper. As I walked past the flamingo pond by the entrance, I could see that they were gathered all standing on one leg as usual, making no sound. This, I thought, was not usual as they don't make much noise anyway but usually there are the ducks clacking in the background.

I went in further but still no sounds, then I turned back to wait for you. Molly has called Cecilia and they should have come in by the back gate and be in the restaurant by now waiting for us.

We have talked about premonitions in an abstract way, but there was something here that went way beyond that. A sense of despair, I could not describe it adequately. We reached the restaurant and both Cecilia and Molly were very quiet.

'What do you think is going on?' said Cecilia.

'I don't know,' I lied, as I had an idea forming in my mind. I knew by some instinct that I had to check the island and by the same instinct, I rather knew what I might find.

'Joe, will you come with me?' I asked. 'You two stay here.'

'Lead on,' said Joe, and by the look on his face, I saw the same despair that I felt.

We took an abnormally long time untying the boat, putting the oars in the rowlocks and pushing off. Everything seemed, including us, to be happening in slow motion. The feeling of dread deepened. Then, out of the silence, a sound, it began with a deep soft hooting and quickly rose to a shrieking primeval wail from the gibbons. It was not our presence, they were used to that, it was something else.

We docked the boat and clambered out. We did not have to search. We both knew what we were about to find. There on the floor of the main hut, lay Larry. Thinner, dirty and very,

very still. I didn't even need to check his pulse. I knew he was dead. And I laid him out on the hut floor. He was still warm. He had only been dead a short while. The animals knew he was there. Knew he was dying. That was what the noise was all about and then they fell silent.

Now the grief and it was catching and flew around the zoo like wildfire. Not the huge cacophony of sound as before but plaintiff cries. Joe and I cried too.

'Can we come across,' shouted Molly, 'what have you found? It's Larry, isn't it?'

We went to fetch them and they came and knelt by the boy. 'Poor soul,' said Molly, 'he was so happy with us. He looks emaciated and there are bruises.'

We must go and tell Walt and see what he wants to do. He should be in the office soon. Let's go up there now.'

'Should I stay with him,' said Molly quietly, 'keep him company?'

'The gibbons will look after him. Look, they are gathering around him now, but stay if you like.'

The three of us got into the boat leaving Molly with Larry and the gibbons, docked and walked slowly up the hill to the office building. There was nothing we could say to each other. Mabel was waiting at the door. 'Funny things going on and strange noises,' she said.

'Got some very sad news, Mabel, Larry is back, he is on the island and he passed away a short time ago,' I said.

'Oh my God,' she cried, 'I felt there was something wrong. What happened to him, such a lovely lad?'

'Too early to tell,' I replied, 'Is Walt in?'

'Mr Whitlam is waiting,' she said primly, 'he knows something's up, go straight in.'

We marched in to his office one by one and he could tell by our faces that bad news was in store so we sat down and he waited patiently for one of us to speak.

'Geoffrey,' said Joe after a struggle, 'Larry has returned from wherever he was. He is on the island and he passed away about an hour ago. It looks like he had been held somewhere as he is very thin and bruised. I suspect he escaped and came back to the one place he could call home and maybe the journey was too much for him. Who knows, I don't think we ever shall. Molly is with him.'

'I don't know what to say, 'said Walt, 'he was so happy here. I thought he would be here with us always but it wasn't to be. Best we call an ambulance, he can't stay there. Mabel, I know you are listening, will you call them, please?'

'Yes, Mr Whitlam, right away.'

'When you have done that, will you let Spencer know and Marjorie, please?'

'Spencer already knows. He's here with me,' said Mabel through the door, 'just go on in Spencer, it's not a time to stand on ceremony.'

'Sad news,' said Spencer, 'don't know what else to say, Marjorie will be very upset, she thought a lot of the lad. Me too.'

'I am going back to the island and wait for the ambulance,' I said, 'can't stay here.'

We dawdled back down the hill with heavy hearts and sat on the picnic bench to wait. The ambulance did not take long and the security guys had opened the main gate for them so they could drive in. Two men got out. 'Where is he?' one said.

'On the island over there, there is someone there with him,' said Cecilia.

'How do we get there?' said the same man.

'You don't,' I replied, 'I will fetch him.'

'You can't do that, we have to check him to make sure.'

'Well, you can check him when I carry him back, you can't go there. There are wild monkeys.' *Not the real reason,* I thought to myself, but I could not bear the thought of them, being there.

'OK, but don't tell anybody. 'Ere you keep watch,' he said to his colleague.

Once at the main hut, I gently released Molly's hands from Larry and lifted him. He didn't weigh very much. He was skin and bone was only the look of serenity on his small face that kept me from breaking down altogether.

'Can you row, Molly?'

'Never tried,' she said.

'Good time to start,' I joked. 'It was not funny.

Onshore I handed Larry over to the ambulancemen who went through their normal routine. ''Fraid he's gone,' one said. I was too choked to respond.

We watched the ambulance drive off in silence.

'Time to get to work,' said Joe, 'keep busy. Best thing.'

'Anyone wants breakfast,' said Molly.

'No, thanks,' we said in unison.

Later that day, we heard that Marjorie had arrived, so we went to meet her at the office.

'Of all the terrible things to happen. At least he got back here where he must have felt safe. He must have been through a terrible ordeal. I have just been to the hospital and I have formally identified him to save you that anyway,' she said, 'I had a brief word with the doctor and he is convinced that he had heart failure due to malnutrition. Too early to tell what to put on the certificate. I'm so sorry.'

'Thanks, Marjorie, give us a call when you know some more.'

'Of course,' replied Marjorie.

The rest of that day and in fact, that week, dragged horribly. Larry's death had left a huge vacuum even more than his enforced absence. That had been easier to cover up from questions by the press but now we were going to have to think of something else to mask his death or be faced with unending probes.

Cecilia came up with the suggestion. 'Why don't we build on what we made up before? Larry has gone back to his homeland and will be working there in a very remote area with endangered species. He feels that that is where he can do most good but will miss this zoo and all the friends he has made here.'

'Cecilia, my love, you have missed your calling, even I could swallow that.'

Three days later, I got a call to the office. Joe and Molly were already there and Cecilia followed through the door minutes after. Marjorie had arrived with Spencer in tow.

212

'Hi everyone,' she said, 'this is going to be difficult. I have the death certificate for you, Joe and Molly, and we will talk about that afterwards. The cause of death is pneumonia leading to heart failure.

'I have seen your press releases which were very well thought out, by the way, but now I have a problem. We have a young boy that nobody has claimed and his whole identity has been made up. Everyone thinks now that he has gone abroad and I think it is best that way otherwise there are going to be a lot of difficult questions. I have gone out on a limb on this one to deal with an exceptional and unique set of circumstances.

'I am going to take a massive gamble and destroy all records we have on him which are, thankfully, not much. Then we have the problem, what do we do with Larry. The doctor, luckily, is a friend of mine and Larry is down as a "John Doe" meaning he has no identity.'

'It is for Joe and Molly to decide,' I said, 'but my vote would be that we should rest him in the place he loved the most. On the island.'

'We agree,' said Joe on behalf of Molly.

And that is what happened. Walt closed the zoo, on the pretext of a gas leak and all but us few went home.

Joe and I dug the grave ourselves during the night and we laid him in a cardboard box in it. Once covered, we fetched Cecilia and Molly while the others watched from the shore. Walt, Mabel, Spencer, Marjorie, Freddy, Emily and the Professor. Among the trees, I think I got a glimpse of Jeremiah and his family but it may just have been my imagination.

Then we left the island to Larry and his best friend, the gibbons sitting with us silently around his unmarked grave.

'Should we say something?' said Cecilia.

'He was a child of God,' whispered Molly, 'maybe the world was not really ready for him.'

Amen.

Epilogue

It is now two years since Larry left us if we could even call it that. Nearly every morning when the weather is fine, we take our one-year-old daughter, Lara, to the island we call our Avalon. Lara is just starting to walk, well toddle, and the very sight of the little boat and the island beyond sends her into shouts of exuberant joy. She has red, auburn hair like her mother, captivates everyone and everything including the animals she meets.

The gibbons see us coming but probably hear her first and line up on the bank waiting for our arrival. We dock, lift Lara onto the bank and she is immediately whisked away by two of the adults. They climb the big tree carrying her upwards and she screams with delight. We are not worried. She is safe. We know and we can feel it.

As for us, we make our way to the little clearing and sit cross-legged for a few moments where the boy rests. Gradually, the colony comes to join us one by one until we are as a whole, linked together not in sound but by a gift which he left for us.

Professor, I think you were wrong. This was something different to autism; it is unfathomable yet very simple.

Cecilia and I know, we talk to each other, but not with words. It is a kind of gift from Larry.

You reading this may call it magic. We have no name for it. We do not need one.